Renata Adler's SPEEDBOAT

"A brilliant series of glimpses into special oddities and new terrors of contemporary life—abrupt, direct, painful and altogether splendid."
—*Donald Barthelme*

"A work of unusual interest...fastidiously lucid, neatly and openly composed."
—*Elizabeth Hardwick*, THE NEW YORK REVIEW OF BOOKS

"Paragraph by paragraph, vignette by vignette, *Speedboat* hilariously builds an unsettling case."
—TIME

"Renata Adler has established herself as a cultural critic notable for the verve and clarity of her style and the brilliance and idiosyncrasy of her observations."
—SATURDAY REVIEW

"This wonderful, funny, courageous book haunts my dreams....Small, perceptibly imperfect...not the kind of book established cultural critics are wont to shout about or display more than relative enthusiasm for. All right, then. *Sotto voce:* Buy, read."
—*Eliot Fremont-Smith*, THE VILLAGE VOICE

SPEEDBOAT

Vintage Books
A Division of Random House
New York

SPEEDBOAT

Renata Adler

First Vintage Books Edition, October 1984
Copyright © 1971, 1972, 1973, 1975, 1976 by Renata Adler
All rights reserved under International and Pan-American
Copyright Conventions. Published in the United States by
Random House, Inc., New York, and simultaneously in
Canada by Random House of Canada Limited, Toronto.
Originally published by Random House, Inc., in 1976.
Much of the material in this book appeared originally,
in slightly different form, in *The New Yorker.*
Library of Congress Cataloging in Publication Data
Adler, Renata.
Speedboat.
Reprint. Originally published: 1st ed. New York:
Random House, c1976.
1. Title.
[PS3551.D63S66 1984]   813'.54   84-40226
ISBN 0-394-72753-3 (pbk.)
Manufactured in the United States of America

For A.

"What war?" said the Prime Minister sharply. "No one has said anything to me about a war. I really think I should have been told. . . ."

And presently, like a circling typhoon, the sounds of battle began to return.

EVELYN WAUGH, *Vile Bodies*

CONTENTS

SPEEDBOAT

CASTLING

Nobody died that year. Nobody prospered. There were no births or marriages. Seventeen reverent satires were written —disrupting a cliché and, presumably, creating a genre. That was a dream, of course, but many of the most important things, I find, are the ones learned in your sleep. Speech, tennis, music, skiing, manners, love—you try them waking and perhaps balk at the jump, and then you're over. You've caught the rhythm of them once and for all, in your sleep at night. The city, of course, can wreck it. So much insomnia. So many rhythms collide. The salesgirl, the landlord, the guests, the bystanders, sixteen varieties of social circumstance in a day. Everyone has the power to call your whole life into question here. Too many people have access to your state of mind. Some people are indifferent to dislike, even relish it. Hardly anyone I know.

"It is only stupid to put up the sails when the wind is against," the wife of the Italian mineral-water tycoon said, on the deck of their beautiful schooner, which had remained all the summer in port. "Because then you lose them."

A large rat crossed my path last night on Fifty-seventh Street. It came out from under a wooden fence at a vacant lot near Bendel's, paused for traffic, and then streaked across to the uptown sidewalk, sat awhile in the dark, and vanished. It was my second rat this week. The first was in a Greek restaurant where there are lap-height sills under all the windows. The rat ran along the sills, straight toward, then past me.

"See that?" Will said, sipping from his beer glass.

"Large mouse," I said. "Even nice hotels have small mice now, in the bars and lobbies." I had last seen Will in Oakland; before that, in Louisiana. He does law. Then something, perhaps a startled sense of my own peripheral vision, registered on my left, coming toward my face fast. My fork clattered.

"You were all right, there," Will said, grinning, "until you lost your cool."

The second rat, of course, may have been the first rat farther uptown, in which case I am either being followed or the rat keeps the same rounds and hours I do. I think sanity, however, is the most profound moral option of our time. Two rats, then. Cabdrivers can't even hear directions through those new partitions, which don't seem to me really bulletproof, although, of course, I've never checked it. Soundproof. One's fingers jam, certainly, in the new receptacles for money. Well, somebody sold the partitions. Someone bought them. Crooked, clearly. There doesn't seem to be a spirit of the times. When I started to get out of bed at an unlikely early morning hour, Will, who pitches into sleep as violently

4

as his waking life is gentle, said, "Just stay here. *Angst* is common." I did find a cab home, in the rain, outside an armory.

"To the Dow-Jones averages," the father said, raising his glass. It was his sixty-eighth birthday. His hair and mustache were silvery.

"Each in his own way," the son said with a little smile. He was not a radical. He had been selling short. They laughed. The entire family—even the grandchildren, at their separate table—drank. The moment passed.

Alone in the sports car, speeding through the countryside, I sang along with the radio station, tuned way up. Not the happiest of songs, Janis Joplin, not in any terms; but one of the nicest lines. "Freedom's just another word for nothing left to lose." In a way, I guess.

"There are no tears here," the young construction worker said at the funeral, when the ancient union leader, with two strokes, three heart attacks, and a lung condition, died at last.

"True," the priest said, surveying the mourners in the cathedral. "No tears. Either the wake went on too long or he was a hard, hard man."

"The rest are never going to die," a young black politician said with great bitterness. "You see them staggering out of their limousines. All Irish, all senile, all strokes. The union men. Even their wives have cardiac conditions. But I know it now. They are never going to die."

"They'll die, all right," the priest said, judiciously. "There's not one of them under seventy-six. You'll see. Your time will come."

"To the future, then," the black politician said.

"Shall we go to your place or to Elaine's?" the young man asked. It was 3 A.M. He was recently divorced. The same question must have been being put just then in cabs throughout New York. "To Elaine's," I said. That was where we went. To Elaine's, to the Dow-Jones averages, to the future, then, to preserve the domestic tranquillity. Freedom means nothing left; cab change receptacles are hearing aids in which one's fingers jam—when the clips are coming in quite fast, it's like waking up and trying to orient the bed. Which side can the wall be on, which side is uptown, downtown, which town is it, anyway? In some of the best motels, near airports, along highways, they have Magic Fingers, a device which, for one quarter put into a metal box, shakes the bed for sixty seconds and sends you quietly to sleep. There are no fingers about it. It is more like sleeping on a train when the tracks are good. A sticker on the metal box says that you can have Magic Fingers in your own home. I don't know anyone who has.

I work for a tabloid, the *Standard Evening Sun.* Since I got this job, I have gone out with four sons of famous fathers, two businessmen with unfinished novels, three writers with a habit of saying "May I use that" when I said something that seemed to them in character, and a revolutionary editor who patted my hair and said "You're very sweet" whenever I asked him anything. I have sat, shivering on cold steps, with a band of fifteen radicals of whom ten were in analysis and six wore contact lenses. Things have changed very much, several times, since I grew up, and, like everyone in New York except the intellectuals, I have led several lives and I still lead some of them.

For a while, I thought I had no real interests—no theater, concerts, museums, stamp collections. Only ambitions and ties to people, of a certain intensity. Different sorts of people. I was becoming a ward heeler of the emotional life. Now the ambitions have drifted after the interests. I have lost my sense of the whole. I wait for events to take a form. I remember somebody saying, "You've got to *steep* yourself in things." So I *steeped* myself, in thrillers, commercials, news magazines. The same person used to write "tepid" and "arguable" all over the margins of what our obituary writers wrote. I now think "tepid" and "arguable" several times a day.

In the country, where I grew up, there were never so many events. Things never went quite so flat. The house was nearly always asleep and we spoke very low. When Father got up at six for his ride or his swim before breakfast, the children, having gone to bed well after midnight, were sleeping. When he came back from his office at noon, the children, pale and silent, joined him for his lunch and their breakfast. After lunch, Father had his nap, and at three Mother, having seen him off again to the office, went upstairs to rest for an hour. The family was awake and together only at supper, after which Father went to his room and Mother stayed downstairs a few minutes to talk to the children. Twenty hours out of twenty-four, in short, the hush of sleep lay over the house. Nobody thought of waking anybody. Sometimes a stupid child would tie a firecracker to a crayfish or a frog just once, and light the fuse. Or give a piece of sugar to a raccoon, which in its odd fastidiousness would wash that sugar in a brook till there was nothing left.

But here. I used to wonder why the victims of some small sensational tragedy—the parents of a little girl who had just been thrown from the roof of her tenement by a deranged older boy, or the family of a model son who had just gone clear out of his mind and murdered a friend—never shut the door in my face when I came for an interview. They never do. They open the door; they bring out the family album and the baby anecdotes. I used to think it was out of a loyalty to memory, or a will to have the papers get it right. I still think it's partly that, and partly being stunned by publicity and grief. But now I know it's mostly an agony of trying to please, a cast of mind so deep and amiable that it is as stark in consciousness as death.

In the matter of Doberman pinschers, I like dogs that are large and hairy and friendly and sleep a lot, with sad eyes behind the hair. When I was young, there was a lady on our road who had a Doberman pinscher, bred sharp, vicious, and streamlined, as they all are, like a honed wolf. It meant that whenever a neighborhood child was riding along the tar road on his bicycle, if the Doberman was out, there had to be an immediate leap from the bicycle, and a crouching on bruised knees behind a high stone wall, before the owner called her dog back. The dog was devoted to the lady, who, as it happened, did have cancer. For years, I thought of the devotion of Dobermans to their owners, and their savagery to others, as something almost in their favor. Almost. Then I read a newspaper story about a Doberman that had turned, after many years, upon its mistress, an old lady. When they found her the next morning, it turned out that the lady must have run from room to room, trying to shut the door before the dog got to her, just too feeble or perhaps unbelieving to escape it. A love story gone off the tracks, one could say in a disillusioned moment. Far off.

From time to time, I work with Will at the foundation, rewriting requests for grants. No such job technically exists, but that's what I do. I try to recycle the film-is-the-medium and the cable-television-for-the-ghetto people, and help the Blake fanatics and the street reformers who work very hard. Sometimes I miss, or lose, the point. Late-sleeping utopians, especially, persist like mercury. I am a fanatic myself, although not a woman of temperament. I get nervous at scenes. I stole a washcloth once from a motel in Angkor Wat. The bellboy was incensed. I had to give it back. To promote the general welfare and secure the blessings of liberty to ourselves and our posterity—I believe all that. I go to parties almost whenever I am asked. I think a high tone of moral indignation, used too often, is an ugly thing. I get up at eight. Quite often now I have a drink before eleven. In some ways, I have overshot my mark in life in spades.

I was lying on a Mediterranean boat deck, on a windless day. It was odd that I should be there, but no more odd than my work, or the slums, or the places where people do find themselves as their luck shifts. A girl of eighteen was taking the sun with great seriousness. The rest of our party were swimming, or playing cards below, or drinking hard. The girl was blond, shy, and laconic. After two hours of silence, in that sun, she spoke. "When you have a tan," she said, "what have you got?"

I have zoomed around a lot in the brief times between months of idling. I have a tendency to get stuck in places. In spring, 1967, I was stuck in Luxor, Egypt. I had been sent to Cairo by the paper. There were loudspeakers and angry rallies in the streets. I went to the pyramids and rode a camel. Then, I went to a briefing at the embassy. The foreign minister spoke of Israeli options and attrition. I wrote it down. I took a plane, an Ilyushin, to Luxor and looked at the tombs there. I arrived for my flight back to Cairo three hours early. So did others. We were told that our flight had been taken over by an American Bible-tour group called "Nine Days in the Holy Land," whose own flight had been cancelled. The scheduled people with reservations were all planeless. I was frantic. I began to cry at the desk of an airport official. He wrote it down. One of the Bible tour's two leaders said that if a single person from his group was left off the plane the tour would never again come to Egypt. I wondered where else they were going to take their "Nine Days in the Holy Land" to. Anaheim, Azusa, Cucamonga. I was desperate. The Egyptian pilot looked at me a second. Just before takeoff, he led me to the cockpit, where I sat, with one of the group's two guides, beside him. The threatening tour guide had been left behind. We flew with a certain exhilaration. A few days after that, there was the war.

I know someone who is trying to get rid of a myna bird —I mean, find a loving owner. For a year now, he has spent half an hour each day underneath a dark cloth with the bird and a timer. He says hello, hello, hello for the entire session. The bird says nothing. It sometimes squawks at sunrise. Then there is the question of apartments. Lucas, who has the desk beside mine at the paper, moved into a place where the last tenant somehow left a lonely cat. Lucas is one of the nicest people I know; he has an allergy to cat hairs. He called everyone he knew. Finally, he heard of someone who already had four cats. He called her. "Well, you see, I already have four cats," the girl said. "I know," Lucas answered. He just thought maybe a fifth . . . "No, no," the girl said. "I mean four *extra* cats. Somebody gave me." There was a pause. "Oh, what the hell," she said. Lucas brought the ninth cat over. Next door, there is a twelve-year-old who wants to give her rabbit to somebody with a happy home out in the country. She is obsessed with the idea that the wrong kind of person might take the rabbit in bad faith and eat it. She thinks somebody ate her gerbil. No one eats gerbils. It is strange to think that most of the children under six whom one knows and loves, gives presents to, whatever, are not going to remember most emotional events of those first years, on the couch, or in jail, or in a bank, wherever they may find themselves when they are twenty-five.

I have been lucky, in my work, at getting visas to closed places. My family have all kept fresh, renewed passports ever since my parents left Europe before the war. Paul-Ernst was my father's name when he was German. It became Pablo when he bought a Costa Rican passport. He was Paulo when we all became Italians in Lugano. Now he's Paul on nights when he, improbably, plays poker. My own mind is a tenement. Some elevators work. There are orange peels and muggings in the halls. Squatters and double locks on some floors, a few flowered window boxes, half-dressed bachelors cooling on the outside fire steps; plaster falls. Sometimes it seems that this may be a nervous breakdown—sleeping all day, tears, insomnia at midnight, and again at four A.M. Then it occurs to me that a lot of people have it. Or, of course, worse. There was the time I had blue triangles on the edges of my feet. Triangles, darker every day, isosceles. I thought, leukemia. I waited a few days and watched. It turned out that whenever I, walking barefoot, put out the garbage on the landing, I held the apartment door open, bending over from the rear. The door would cross a bit over the tops of my bare feet. That was all—triangle bruises. I took a little celebrational nap.

"I yield to myself," the congressman said, at the start of the speech with which he was about to enter history, "as much time as I will consume."

He was on the phone. I will ask her to dinner, he thought. I will accept her invitation to a party. I will laugh at whatever seems to constitute a joke in her mind, if she will only permit me, with the pact of affection still securely in our voices, to hang up. She continued to talk through her end of the phone, though. When he sounded unamused, her voice seemed to reproach him. When he tried an animated tone, she seemed encouraged to continue. She kept patting every sentence along the line with a little crazy laugh.

I don't know how many people have ever seen or passed through Broadway Junction. It seems to me one of the world's true wonders: nine crisscrossing, overlapping elevated tracks, high in the air, with subway cars screeching, despite uncanny slowness, over thick rusted girders, to distant, sordid places. It might have been created by an architect with an Erector Set and recurrent amnesia, and city ordinances and graft, this senseless ruined monster of all subways, in the air. Not far away, there is that Brownsville section of crushed, hollowed houses, an immense metropolis in ruins, with an occasional junkie, corpse, demented soul intent upon an errand where no errand can exist. There can't even be rats, unless they're feeding on each other. Then, just on the edge of this deserted strangeness, there begins a little neighborhood of sorts, with tenants, funeral homes, groceries, one or two policemen. Once, along the border street, I saw an endless line of Cadillacs, with men in suits and hats, with chauffeurs and manicures and somber faces. An owner of a liquor store had passed on to the funeral home. The Italians who run that community were paying their respects. The actual street neighbors seemed divided between obligations to the dear departed and protocols toward the men in Cadillacs. Nothing for the foundation here. Nothing for the paper, either. No events.

"Any dreams?" the doctor asked his patient softly, tentatively, as we used to say in the child's card game, "Any aces? Any tens?"

In actual fact, the lady on the Boeing 707 from Zurich was talking to me about seaweed. I had just come from St. Moritz and she from Gstaad. Nearly all the other passengers were in casts from skiing. Her husband had invented a calorie-free spaghetti made from seaweed. He had invented other seaweed products, including a seaweed sauce for the spaghetti. He was the world's yet unacknowledged living authority on seaweed and its many uses. She was quite eloquent about it. I was interested for nearly seven hours. My capacity for having a good time exists. It surfaces, however, on odd occasions. Everybody's capacity for having a good time. It must have been fun before the casts, and there will always be another season. The man who hurls himself in order to be the last person through the closing doors of an already overcrowded subway pushes, after all, some timid souls in front of him. Maybe the stresses of winding toward the millennium.

"Well, you know. His wife was chased by an elephant."
"No."
"How extraordinary."
"Yes. It was too awful. They were watching the elephants, when she simply fell down. The elephant ran over and knelt on her. She was in the hospital for months."
"No."
"How extraordinary."
"Quite different from anything she ever got from Roger, I expect."

Day after day, when I still worked at the Forty-second Street branch of the public library, I saw the same young man, bearded, intense, cleaning his fingernails on the corners of the pages of a book. "What are you studying for?" I asked him once. The numbers were flashing over the counter as the books came up. "Research," he said. "I'm writing my autobiography." There are certainly odd people in that reading room—one who doodles the same bird endlessly on the back of a half of a single bank check, one who hums all the time, and one who keeps asking the other two to stop. A little pantomime concerto. I quit that job soon. The trouble is, I sometimes understand that research project. Or I did understand it. Then.

"What a riot!" a girl of about twenty-five, not thin, exclaimed as the de Havilland Otter started down the runway of the Fishers Island airport. "Is this a toy or an airplane?" a young man with a sparse mustache asked nervously. "I paid for my ticket twice. They pulled the Fishers Island–New York section by mistake, in Groton. Now there's this."
"It's all right," I said. "I was in a plane like this when I was studying crisis conditions in Southeast Asia. They have

outhouses behind their huts, over the rivers. Then they eat the river carp. Ecology. Everyone trusted these planes. The worry was just bombs and mortars. They seemed most concerned about the local cockfights. Gamecocks. I had never seen one till I went there. Ben Tre. It no longer exists. For flights I have these pills."

"The Wright Brothers' special," the Fishers Island girl continued. A clattering began under the floor of the plane's midsection. All ten passengers started their own tones of laughter. The clattering was overlaid with creaking. "Can you believe it?" the girl said. "It's fantastic."

"The most fun is when you hit the clouds and have to pedal," a sailor said. He was stationed in Groton. The plane incessantly jarred, bounced, and tilted. I counted and found I had enough painkilling pills for everyone. "I always pack too much whenever I travel," a lady said quite loudly as the windows fogged. "We're moving from New York. My son has been mugged six times. He's just eleven. We can't keep buying him new watches." She went on like that. The two-ticket man held on to my wrist so tightly that my own watch left marks for hours after, on the white ring watches leave inside a tan. We landed at LaGuardia. The young man let go.

Another weekend. Any dreams. P.O. Box 1492.

The school was run by Communists, although few parents were aware of that. The grades ran from one to twelve. The younger children slept throughout the year on a screened-in open porch that was thought, in wintertime, to confer immunities. There were sixteen double-decker beds on the porch, and one single bed, near the door, for the child who was held to be the most disturbed in any given year. Late at night, the oldest told horror stories. Later still, the most disturbed child would bang her head against the bedpost in her sleep, or cry, or speak in no known language, whatever the disturbance that year was. Before dawn, the rest leaped wildly from top bunk to top bunk, sometimes single file,

14

sometimes racing, sometimes three leapers side by side at a single time. Once or twice in those years, somebody crashed and broke a leg.

We voted constantly on everything—issues and offices of every kind. We were expected at every age to have an opinion on all matters, political matters in particular. Although pressure from the teachers that year was clearly for Wallace (Henry, not George), the teachers restrained themselves— nominally because they valued our independent judgment, actually because they lived in dread of our petitions. We fired a housemother by petition. We voted in fifth-grade physics that half a pound of feathers weighed more than half a pound of steel. We were adamant. Knowledge itself was a democracy. We studied fanatically. We were as competitive as only a child state can be. We voted to stone the girl who banged her head—not because she banged her head, but because she was so fat and furtive and whining all the time. She lost a loafer running from us across the athletic field. None of the stones hit. We were too uncoördinated and too young to throw accurately across the distance we had also, in all fairness, voted for. The space-time continuum became clear to us with that event. So, perhaps, did the quality of mercy, after all. We did not vote to fire the shop teacher, although we wanted to. We planed and sawed and used the lathe and soldered, making Christmas presents for our families. Christmas in all wildly progressive schools was celebrated with obsessional gravity. In one year's holy pageant, a girl's hair caught fire, from a candle held reverently by the boy behind. A father leaped to the balcony and put the fire out. Parents were allowed to visit every other Sunday, and for pageants and plays.

Excellent evidence. "The source said that the investigators considered the responses of the dogs 'excellent evidence,'" the *Times* reported. "In each case the two dogs reacted positively to Mr. Hoffa's scent. One by standing up," the story went on, "and the other by sitting down." Since Will is a lawyer and I used to be an investigative reporter, we conclude that the dogs went to different schools, one to a sitting school, one to a standing school, but anyway to different schools.

There were, of course, in all such places, compulsory classes in ballet. Boys and girls, in leotards, lying around the resined floor in ballet class, were all instructed to listen, eyes shut, to Chopin or the Firebird or something, and let the mind run freely over whatever the music might suggest, all enjoined particularly to relax. The music played. Pensive children mused. Ambitious children worried. Homesick children grieved. Everyone lay still. Suddenly, the ballet teacher would swoop down and pick up somebody's hand or foot. Newcomers were often startled into a small scream. After the first few times, they regained control. Determined then to show just how relaxed they were, they would obligingly help to raise the swooped-at hand or foot, try even to anticipate the swoop. "Why, you're not relaxed," the teacher—quite commonly a psychology major, born in Riverdale and recently divorced from an Algerian or Pakistani—would say, in astonishment and reproach. "Look at it. Why, just look at this foot." She would hold the foot a moment, and then let it go. For normally nervous children, there were two possibilities: being left with a raised foot; or being just alert enough to let it drop, not limply, however, as it was meant to fall, but like a stone. In either case, in the name, it seemed, of dance, the teacher would deal in earnest with that hand or foot; and if you did not have a nervous breakdown then, you had presumably acquired—as from that wintry open porch; as, for that matter, from being sent away to boarding school at the age of six or eight—another immunity. It was always, of course, rumored that somebody in these classes, out of pure calm, fell asleep. But like that other, more flamboyant and dangerous story, which was told in public schools —that some child had lain down between the railroad tracks in town, and had remained there, relaxed and unharmed, while all the cars of a train passed over him—it was a fable. It was false.

"I'm sorry. Mr. Ellis has stepped out. He's on another line. He's in a meeting. Mrs. Harwell? Oh, just a minute. She's away from her desk."

There is a particular fanaticism about riding in progressive summer camps and prep schools. The camps may sound either drawn from Hiawatha, or like a condition that will require surgery—my brothers went to Melatoma, I to Sighing Rock. The schools will be named for an improbable condition of the landscape (Peat Cliff, Glen Willow Sands, Mount Cove, Apple Valley Heights), or for something dour and English: Gladstone Wett. The riding teachers are named Miss Cartwright, Miss Farew, Martha Abbott Struth. Ms. Struth, if she is married, will have her own academy, which teaches every horse thing from gymkhana to dressage. Mr. Struth has been away or dead for twenty years. Field hockey coaches, whistles hanging from their necks, brown and white oxfords on their feet, may stride, with their emphatic, shoulder-inflected hockey walk; they can shout, exhort, scold, shrilly whistle, keep a red and frosty silence, like their counterparts on football fields. All field coaches carry on—as though those fractures, scars, grunts, knockouts, limps, and broken noses were well worth it. Field hockey for girls, football for boys, seeming to them, perhaps, such useful skills to have in adult life. These coaches, male and female, have always had disciples. In fact, I know of no one who was a boarding student at a wildly progressive school, in those years, who did not incur a slight, though permanently laming or disfiguring injury on its fields. But it was horses that held the imagination; it has always been the riding teachers who preside.

At that school, sex and mysticism set in, simultaneously. We used to walk through the dark, from our porch, to the stables, where we imagined that a horse had died, untended and alone. We had not been told. Couples, late at night, holding hands, looking for the corpse of Gladys—who had, in fact, been sold, the school having fallen on hard times. We slept in the hay above the stalls. We returned to our porches before dawn. The school has since gone entirely to seed— heroin, LSD, precocious abortions, methedrine. In our time, we planned but did not even dare to run away. We had codes, ceremonies, aliases. We had oaths. We had marathon walks and rides. Once, on the morning of the middle children's all-day ride, with the night to be spent in sleeping bags, a matter of great ritual importance to us then, a small girl from a theatrical family said to us, in parting, "Break a leg." We had a unison of panic. Superstition had become intense.

Myra Miller broke a leg. It was my fault. I had a dread by then of our most skittish, lightest horse. It always seemed, in his nervousness and mine, that I was gliding on unsteady air. I was assigned that horse. The first time he shied—at a flower, I think—I fell off, deliberately. Myra, who had been given the phlegmatic nag I longed for, took advantage of the flash of fear to spur that nag, for the first time in its ten horse years, no doubt, to gallop through the woods, with frightened eyes. Myra gave a rebel yell, and used a switch. The nag galloped too close by a tree, which, like Absalom's, singled Myra out—not by the hair but by the leg. Her leg was broken by the time she fell. I was left with her while the rest of the expedition went for help. "Anything I can do?" I kept saying. Myra would say, "Oh, Christ." I have since heard this precise exchange many times, out here.

Then Myra's mother came. Not a play, or pageant, or Sunday—Myra's accident. The mother and I talked. There was a bath schedule outside the porch bathroom—each child having been allotted an uncapitalist three baths a week. "I have to go to the loo," Myra's mother said. She tried to commit suicide in there. Not very seriously. With nail scissors. "It's my fault," she kept saying, when the ambulance came. "Myra's all my fault." That was probably true. The fault for the leg was mine. I rode, on the school's insistence, the same skittish horse all term after that. I reined him back till his mouth was wrecked for the snaffle, and the curb was all that would hold him back. The riding teacher used to throw stones at him to make him go. When he went, I would fall off at once.

Ten years ago, I was in Mississippi, covering blacks, whites, troopers, Klansmen, nuns, whoever there was. The F.B.I. had already infiltrated the Klan to the extent that, by whatever means, they had demoralized and almost destroyed it. A small-town klavern, run by a gas-station attendant, did discover an agent in their midst. They drove him to a dark, deserted road. He conceded that they'd caught him. His predicament was trouble. He also promised that, if they did him any harm whatever, some other agents at the Bureau would come down and blow the Klansmen's heads off. They did nothing to him. That klavern dispersed. Later, when there still seemed to be an obdurate nest of Klansmen left in Mississippi and Louisiana, it was rumored that some F.B.I. men, having tried all sorts of warnings and persuasions, drove a few of the unrelenting to another rural road and blew their heads off. It may not be true. Agents from that time and place will just grin when they are asked.

She was a dynamite girl and he was an aces fellow. On the day he at last agreed by phone to marry her, the switchboard operators were overjoyed. For six months they had listened, in sympathy and indignation, to the tears, the threats, the partings and reconciliations. They were so unequivocally for the girl that only the purest professionalism kept them, at times, from breaking in. On the day Tim, after calls to his best friend, his first wife, and his therapist, gave in at last, the oldest operator, who had been on the switchboard for twenty years, actually wept. The other two told the receptionist, at lunch. All four ladies had a drink, and then bought a card of slightly obscene felicitations. They had wavered toward the sentimental, but rejected it as basically unswinging. They

did not sign the card. Tim and his girl, who had been breaking up once again on the day they received it (she was pack-
ing; they were in his apartment), were appalled. As a result
of the card, and discussions of what to do about it—what it
implied, who knew and who didn't—they married.

A physicist I first met when he was working on a government military project recently turned to drastic civil
disobedience. When I went to visit him and his wife in their
Village apartment, the phone rang constantly—two rings for
one sort of friend, ten for another. "If it took an act that I
might go to jail for to bring my friends together for an
evening," the physicist said, "then it wasn't pointless, was
it?" The apartment was filled with friends from other days,
other lives, looking tired and talking. The doorbell kept on
ringing. A young priest would go downstairs and check.
"Who was that?" the physicist said when the priest came
back alone. "A man from the *Daily News,*" the priest said.
"I told him you weren't here." A reader of the *News* ob-
jected. "They had a petition protesting their own coverage of
this kind of story. Maybe he signed it." The physicist was out
the door and halfway down the block in a minute. He came
back. "I found the guy," he said. "I asked him whether he
signed. He said no, he felt he could do more by not signing,
by positive action in covering just this kind of story. I
thanked him. I asked him to convey my thanks to the people
who did sign. The guy said, I'm sure they would appreciate
it more if you wrote them a personal note. I said, Oh, no, I
feel I can do more by positive action in just this kind of
conversation."

When I first came to New York, a man I somehow knew,
a film producer, took me from my job at the school where
I was then working to dinner at the Colony. Before dinner,
I was to meet him at his St. Regis suite. I arrived ten minutes
late and knew at once it was an error. I should have waited
twenty minutes. I had just started smoking weeks before.

20

Over drinks in the suite, he lighted my cigarette. The match fell on the rug. I picked it up. Another error. He was a nice man. After dinner, he walked me up all six flights of the place where I was living. "It's been so long since I've seen a girl's apartment," he said. After a while, there was one of those awkward, off-romantic moments. "It's not my age, is it?" he said, earnestly. He was seventy-four. "No, no," I said, "I guess I'm just neurotic." That seemed all right. We became friends. At one point, he thought I might be the girl for his son, another film producer. It was awkward for the son and me, at Trader Vic's, trying to be a generation. The son said he had three files of projects: one marked A through Z; one A prime through Z prime; and one marked Miscellaneous. He said that only since his analysis had he come to realize how much he had to offer.

The line stuck with me, though—I guess I'm just neurotic. Nothing else seemed to work quite so well, to be so serviceable and friendly. You don't care to. I don't care to. It isn't a New York obligation. There's already somebody. I don't like the way you talk to waiters. I'm not an agency. You're not an agency. Whatever. Being neurotic seemed to be a kind of wild card, an all-purpose explanation. Other ways, of course, are straighter. I don't know. An old friend—the physicist, in fact, before he married—once told me that a sister of a friend of his had sexual problems. I said, oh. He said that, when they had both been in Bolivia at a meeting, he'd made a pass at her. She wasn't interested. He asked her why. She said "You just don't attract me physically." That was it. For him, the inference was problems. Maybe there is no polite way. There don't seem to be many instances of the pure straightforward. And yet. Will is away a lot. I have my work. There is a passage in Dante when he and Virgil, travelling through the Inferno, stop beside a man buried to his neck in boiling mud. He does not care to speak to them. He has his own problems. He does not want an interview. Dante actually grasps him by the hair and gets his story. Some sort of parable about reporting there, I think. In fact, I know.

In May, 1959, Bootsy Garn, from Houston, Texas, refused to get out of the bus near Stroudsburg, Pennsylvania. Her hair was shiny and blond. Her nails were extremely long and red. She was wearing silk trousers and pumps. She looked at her fellow students in sneakers and jeans, with their canvas sacks and pickaxes, and at the slate cliffs they seemed prepared to go straight up. She declined. "I just don't see the sense of it," she said. Bootsy got off the bus all three nights, did her nails, set her hair, and slept in the dingy hotel above the movie house with the rest of us. She was by no means one of the great refusers. Not an existentialist hero, or a Rosa Parks, or even a Bartleby. She simply did not see the sense of it. It would have been an outrage, even in the highest traditions of scholarship, to force Bootsy too far into the out-of-doors. She knew it, and she kept her dignity. In 1959.

She spent the three days of that field trip aboard the bus. She nearly flunked geology, defaulted the science requirement, and lost her college degree. A quiet exception had to be made. She passed. The rest of us climbed the cliffs and hills, looked at entrenched meanders, terminal moraines, glacial detritus, relief maps of the Delaware Water Gap, and outcroppings of the Wissahickon Mica Schist. None of it has since been of much use to me. I can tell an entrenched meander to this day. It means that the riverbed is old and that the river has doubled back to cut its own deep loops. But that's all. I can't tell one rock from the next, or recite ten lines from *Faust,* or recall the whole Preamble, or do one Old Slavonic text. Not one. It is all gone, after childhood knowledge of myths, constellations, baseball scores, dinosaurs, and idioms of the tennis court and athletic field. There are outcroppings of the old vocabularies still. Pinnies from field hockey. Heels down. Bad hop. Sorry. My fault. So sorry. Provide for the common defense. Meanders slip my mind. And of college there is so little, although that little does flare, like the Jesuit poet's embers, gash-gold vermilion, when I remember it at all.

"The score," the megaphone on the ferry around Manhattan said, from time to time, without further explanation, "is one to nothing." To the foreigners, unaware perhaps that a World Series was in progress, this may have seemed an obscure instruction, or a commentary on the sights. "In the top of the fifth," it said, with some excitement, as we rounded Wall Street, "the score is five to one."

When Gregor Imelda from San Diego arrived at the wedding breakfast outside Greenwood, Mississippi, we realized what a mixed group we have become. Imelda itself is not Jones exactly, but we were doing introductions by first names. "Gregor, this is Inge. Inge, Greg. Gregor, Carlo, Didi, Dibo, Idris, Jude, Vlad, Ara, Si, Matt, Dommy, Elio, Gregor. Arne." It sounded like a countdown on Ellis Island, or in Babel. Or one of those nonsense marching chants for the tribes of boys in summer camp. My brothers', I remember, was Hippta, minnega, zinnega, honnega; Zopta bumbalaya hoc. Jude and Vlad are married to each other, which makes it hard to tell just from their names which one is which. Gregor sorted it out. He had eggs and bacon. There was kudzu growing outside the veranda. Beyond that, tall pines and Spanish moss. There were plaques commemorating dead dogs on many flagstones. "Morton, Great Dane, 1937." "Muffie, Spaniel, 1941." Dommy, whose mother was a maid, or a domestic, or whatever they then called it, was uneasy about the blacks, whom we seemed to be calling staff or help. None of us is leading quite the life we were at all prepared for. We were born in Beirut, Boston, Albuquerque, Rome, the Bronx, Antibes, Ontario, Tel Aviv. Vlad is a resident in orthopedic surgery. He has a scar on his hand from the day an eccentric surgeon in a temper slapped him with a scalpel. Some of us are vegetarians. Some drink. Some take pills. It is possible that we have, separately, acquired the capacity to say a qualified No to any going, too going, concern.

23

Dispersed as we all are, though, what we seem to have entirely in common is a time, a quality of meaning no harm, and a sense that among highly urban and ambitious people we are trying to lead some semblance of decent lives. Marriages of the second house break up. A couple may study blueprints for this second house, and build it, or they may buy a farmhouse that is very old. A trailer, or a diner, or a diner *in* a trailer, always seems to materialize across the road from this second house. Even if it doesn't, by the end of summer, wife and children do return to the first house in the city. The husband borrows an apartment or moves to a hotel. Not in every case, of course. In a lot of cases. None of us is, however, at all one of those stencil bohemians who live in the Village, cultivate for their public lives something leftish and for their private lives a guru or an analyst, who are likely to be by birth and accent New York, and who are likely at parties to have somewhere in the room a stereo; elsewhere a baby, pale and whimpering, until its mother, having until last week breast-fed it at just such parties as this one, mashes a little phenobarbital into its bottle and around its pacifier; elsewhere still one large Cuban or Jamaican, who is cooking something difficult, which includes rice and bananas and which, since it is very late and is the only supper, makes it certain that everyone will be joylessly, sickly drunk all evening on the Gallo wine and sangría in paper cups. No. On the other hand, we are all linked to lives of all sorts. Phoebe Aaron, a medieval scholar at our university, used to be listed in the phone book as P. Aaron. She was always being called by heavy breathers. Recently, she moved out to Chicago, as a full professor. She decided to list her full name, Phoebe Aaron. The first time her phone rang in her new place, it was just another breather, Middlewestern. "Hello, Phobe?" he said.

Vlad, who wants to specialize one day in surgery on adult hands, finds himself these days working on babies. There is a relatively new surgical procedure that, if it is performed within fourteen hours of delivery, will keep alive a baby who would otherwise have simply, surely died. After the lifesaving procedure, Vlad gets the baby. He does what he can for it with orthopedic surgery. It is perfect practice for a future with delicate, adult hands. Vlad thinks that, like so many valuable learning experiences, it cannot, cannot in the end ever be or have been worth it. I once saw, however, what might have seemed an altogether hopeless old man on crutches, making his way out of Disneyland, with a large Mickey Mouse balloon.

In Bootsy Garn's final college year, my first, the girl across the hall from me bought a snake. The girl's father had been a famous American fascist in the thirties. It was assumed the girl had problems. But pets were not permitted in the dorms. The college knew nothing of the snake. The girl in the room next door to mine bought an alligator. Her father was head of a chemical corporation in Cincinnati. The girl was beautiful. She held séances. She had an Austrian boyfriend, older than she by enough to have been a true Nazi in his time, who threw stones through her window and shouted "Annelise, Annelise," in a kind of whisper-shout each night while she fed her little alligator halves of worms. Her name, in fact, was Anne. The girls in another dorm bought ducks. The girl three rooms down the hall from me had an orgone box. She believed in silence at breakfast, and used to enforce it by staring craftily at a bread knife with jam on it. An African princess, in her third year and wildly in unrequited love, tried to kill herself one evening by taking an overdose of Epsom salts. She fell in convulsions in front of the dining-room door. Rumors had begun to reach the dean's office. Something amiss. Anne asked me to hide her alligator in my room for a night or two. I thought, This must be college, what the hell. Three nights I heard dry feet and scales dragging forlornly across my floor. The creature missed the damp. I took it to the bathtub in the early-morning hours. The third day, I left it there. Just before nine, the fascist's daughter decided to let it be known that her snake was lost. It must have crawled out through its mesh. She thought it had entered the radiator and was now at large in the heating system. It was a very small snake, red, yellow, and black. Bootsy went straight to her room, locked the door, and screamed. For thirty-six hours, she refused to come out. The rest of us, rather dreading the emergence of the snake from our own radiators, avoided our rooms. Bootsy just stayed, and then, the following evening, came quietly out and took a bath. Neither the alligator nor the snake was seen again. Those of us who were studying the English Drama Until 1642 resumed our course. And now I'm here.

The girl in the hallway of Sam's building, as I was rushing home, was much too fast asleep. She did not look sick. She was not unkempt. She just did not seem entirely alive. "Hey," I said. "Excuse me. Are you all right?" She just sat there, hands clasped in her lap, large purse by her side. A man walked in from the street. "Excuse me," I said. "Does this girl look all right to you?" He looked at her a while. She made no flicker of a move. "Do you know her?" he asked. "No," I said. "Do you?" He shook his head, crossed the hall to the elevator, got in, and was gone. I went back upstairs and rang Sam's bell. I said, "There's something wrong with a girl who's sitting in your hall." Sam came downstairs with me.

"Hey," he said, shaking her shoulder a bit. She just sat there, asleep. Sam took one of her clasped hands, lifted it, and let it drop. "Do you think we should call an ambulance?" I said. "Maybe we should look in her bag first, and see who she is," he said. "Maybe she wouldn't want an ambulance." I said, "If you look in her bag, though, they'll think it has something to do with you." It was the first time I had ever used this sense of "they." We stared at the girl. She woke up. She was all right. She went home.

I think when you are truly stuck, when you have stood still in the same spot for too long, you throw a grenade in exactly the spot you were standing in, and jump, and pray. It is the momentum of last resort. Some people get a jump on the morning in other ways—speeding on the highways, making money, doing crossword puzzles, a darker tan, a whiter wash, accumulations of various kinds. The thing about doing the Sunday crossword is that halfway through you may find yourself tracking a mind you loathe. I begin, like most people, with the gap definitions, "53 Down rara——," and continue with the words I know for sure. I find that if I can manage to fill the upper left-hand corner very early, I am never able to complete the rest. I don't know why. Crosswords start for me in the middle, or they don't work out. I have never been any good at bridge, chess, or Scrabble, either. Some people gain momentum on envy or rage. I tend to blast myself out of bed into situations that are drastically odd, with a moral edge, perhaps, and an element of risk. I took a plane once from an Angolan island of eccentrics to what was then Biafra, on a Joint Church Aid load of fish. In the thunder and lightning, and Valium and a sense of incongruity, it was fine.

There were only three journalists there then, in the penultimate days of Biafran misery. We had been told to bring cans of food, jerry cans of gasoline, and a lot of Scotch. One evening, we drank some of the Scotch in a bungalow, which was several miles from mine. At sunset, I thought I should go home, meaning my bungalow. One of the journalists said he knew the way, even in the dark. We could walk there later. The rain was total. We got lost. I could not quite believe it. Planes overhead somehow. We kept bumping into sentries, who could not believe it, either. Finally, we found my bungalow. I'm out. We're still here. Biafra's not. Before the Six-Day War, I had bought a Patek Philippe watch and a Chanel suit. I don't know why. They had a song on the Biafran roads. "He is dead. Got to bury him. He died in a state of courage. May his soul rest in peace."

The truth, I would like to say here, is as follows. But I can't. In some places, it may already have begun, the war of everybody against everybody, all against all. "The Great Game," the lady philosopher used to say, quoting from Kipling, "is finished when everyone is dead. Not before."

I often wonder about the people who linger over trash baskets at the corners of the city's sidewalks. One sees them day and night, young and old, well dressed, in rags—often with shopping bags—picking over the trash. They pick out newspapers, envelopes. They discard things. I often wonder who they are and what they're after. I approach and cannot ask them. Anyway, they scurry off. Sometimes I think they are writers who do not write. That "writers write" is meant to be self-evident. People like to say it. I find it is hardly ever true. Writers drink. Writers rant. Writers phone. Writers sleep. I have met very few writers who write at all.

I visited the University of California at Santa Cruz once. It was rich, and near the sea, and full of redwoods. The students who did not care to walk to class were conveyed by surreys with fringes. There was no real way to stage a student strike, since most things were permitted. Attendance in the classes was not taken. The only way to be on strike was to attend a class, and wear a black, identifiably striker's armband. The students wanted to strike on behalf of the local people of Santa Cruz—who loathed them. The strike was a boycott of grapes. The students picketed the local stores that sold grapes. The locals bought up all the grapes and waved them in the students' faces. There seemed to be no understanding among anybody. The troopers were there to protect students from club-bearing locals. The students thought the locals were oppressed by troopers. Education, perhaps, in its own way, suffered. "The only way you can get even a quorum of a class here," a professor told me, "is with a class in

Sensitivity Training or Transcendental Meditation." I left soon.

One night, in Paris, during the last days of the Algerian crisis, I was studying in a common room at the Cité Universitaire—where I used to live and where four apparently interchangeable Americans incessantly played bridge. A bomb went off. The explosion was enormous. Windows smashed. Doors fractured. The reception desk blew up. The lights went out. The first words after the thunder and reverberations in the darkness were an imperturbable, incredulous, "Two *hearts.*" Another night, one of the intermittent bridge players wandered, barefoot, into the common room. She was known for her casual, oddly violent Guess Whats. "Guess what," she said. The other players, noticing that even her feet, on the dusty, littered floor, were an uncharacteristic, American high school clean, guessed she was having an affair. No one in that place, that year, except Southern girls and narcissists seemed to wash any more thoroughly than life required. But the Guess Whats always made an immediate claim; they never passed quite safely until someone guessed correctly or everyone gave up. Bathtub running over, pregnancy, expulsion from a Sorbonne class were guessed. Then wisps of smoke were drifting down the corridor. Nobody moved. More guesses. The girl's roommate made three no trump. Then she choked, and guessed a fire from a hot plate underneath a mattress in the room they shared. Correct. The fumes were poisonous. The room had been half smoldering, half in flames. "Oh, Ruth," the girl said, like some reproachful loser in a mindless chess game, "you always guess."

Elaine's was jammed, full of young women looking tired and their escorts, ignoring them in droves, talking to each other, man to man. The bachelor regulars brought a different girl each night or week or so, and then around midnight, dropped them flat. The beauty point was made. The men

29

could talk, of royalties, pot, sex, screenplays, and politics. The girls, left to each other, girl, space, girl, space, girl, space —four girls at most tables and four empty chairs—looked quite vacant, scared. The general male reluctance seemed to be to go to bed. There was also quite a thing about the check. Some regulars appeared to believe that the check did not exist. "Reach for the check," my father said to his sons, in one of his rare speeches of that kind to them. "Whatever happens, make sure that you pay that check." In a family with siblings, there is a constant war of reflexes. Nothing to do with checks—the opposite. A child is sitting there, with a toy or comic book. Flash. Gone. It takes a wary eye and an instant tightening of the grip, or the thing is gone. The gentlemen at the place are flashes with that check. The others —perhaps only children?—always lose or look away.

Matthew, the man I had arrived with, was drinking brandies. I was drinking gin. Suddenly, my zabaglione vanished, cream, cup, strawberry, and all. I had a distinct, an eidetic memory of seeing it there before me. It was gone. I looked for it. Matt looked for it. It was nowhere. Somebody's handbag was on the floor beside my chair. I felt that a whole zabaglione could not have fallen, tidily, into a stranger's handbag. I couldn't search in a stranger's handbag, anyway. We stopped thinking about it. Matthew said that he had been very fat as a small boy. He read a lot. He ate. When he noticed how alarmed his parents were at how fat he was, he obediently laid his chocolate bars aside. Then, his parents were called to the school. It was a friendly, permissive, finger-painting sort of place. There was a huge papier-mâché policeman in the hall. The policeman's knee had begun to erode. Matthew had been eating papier-mâché. He denied it at the time. He is quite slim now.

We have all, of course, had childhoods. I do find that the person with the clearest, least self-serving simply pays. I remembered another Matthew, an unpleasant child. He came from many miles away to our place, where there was a lake with fish. Matthew never caught one. We went trolling from a rowboat, casting from the shore. Sometimes, we used a bamboo pole and worms. We all caught fish but Matthew. He talked. We rowed him. Nothing happened. At first it was a triumph. Then we were embarrassed. Finally, my brothers had a thought. My older brother said that the secret of fishing in that lake was paper bags. Matthew said Oh, as though he had always known it. I rowed. My brothers put half a worm on Matthew's hook—around that, a paper bag, with a fish concealed inside. In a few minutes, Matthew said he thought he had a bite. He reeled in. He was ecstatic with his half-dead perch. We never told him. Last year, I saw that Matthew, with his children, running for office in Chicago. He spoke of his boyhood, fishing, and of that afternoon when he caught that grand pike, casting. No harm in it. Lucky memory on his part; on my brothers', picking up that check.

A girl at our table said she had had to steal two blouses, that afternoon, at Bloomingdale's. She had had no time to wait. "I never used to have to hustle," her escort kept saying bleakly, "till now. Till now." There was a disturbance at the bar. The waiter, a frail man with hair down to his shoulders, held a huge, ill-tempered, and obstreperous writer face down on the floor in a few seconds flat. The whole restaurant grew quiet for a minute, hummed again. The writer began another scuffle. The waiter dragged him out into the street. Squad cars arrived. Most people at the tables went outside to watch, then came back in to talk. Matt took me home. There was some sort of petition, or document, or word of sponsorship lying upstairs on my desk for signing. I am not a signer. I would like to take the high road, if there is a high road. When I went upstairs, I wondered what it was I had meant to do.

QUIET

That slum of the air, the 747, was waiting its turn. The food
had been awful, the babies had wailed, seventy-two headsets
had broken down before the start of the movie. The top third
of the screen was, as usual, cut off at the ceiling. Little air
vents had blown into the passengers' eyes for nine hours;
there had been sneezes all over the aircraft, and cries of
"Salud." The washrooms had broken down halfway through
the flight, also as usual. The stewardess was still walking the
aisles, spraying scent. The waiting-room music, designed for
calm during dangerous minutes, had played during takeoff,
and now began droning for landing. We landed. As always,
the passengers, having felt the squalor, the suspense, the
scale of confinement, applauded when the wheels touched

the ground. Some got to their feet, and were immediately admonished, in terms of great sarcasm, by the purser, that they had no right to stand until the plane had come to a complete stop. The complete stop itself, as usual, was never announced. An escalator had already reversed itself in Oakland, dumping everyone onto a concrete cellar floor. Some of us had been driving those underserviced crates of steel all the agencies now rent as cars. There were smoke inhalations from derailed subways, and fragments of airport hand grenades. There had been so much travel, we knew someone was going to die.

"It is the sirocco," someone said, looking pale on the boat deck, and passing the aspirin. "No, no," the owner of a shore boutique said. "It is the mistral." A deckhand, politely passing Bloody Marys, said he thought it was the tramontana. "Hangovers," the English horseracing columnist said, quite firmly. "Always blame the wind. Depressions." A Frenchman said that, in any case, he had a *grand cafard*.

I found a quarter yesterday, in a puddle, in Wilmington. I have a history of finding coins—a penny on the sidewalk one spring morning on Park Avenue, a dime that afternoon; the next day, on the bus, eleven cents, exactly. It seemed a sign. I have found coins abroad. Leaving aside minor jackpots hit in pay phones (which seem only fair, considering the change one loses when those things are out of order), last month I found a quarter in the back seat of a cab. Nobody saw. I have no regard for the law in these matters, as in several others. By law, I think, it now belonged to the owner of the cab. He was not there. A passenger had clearly lost it. He was gone. In the end, having noticed that the driver of the cab was black, I gave it up. I said, "Excuse me. I think you have lost this quarter." He said, "Thanks." An old friend, who teaches, these days, at a seminary, had the fine solution. He said I should have given a different quarter to the driver, kept the one I found. I wish I'd thought of it. I find that many city people give their most minute attention to the ethics of found objects, small.

It is not even that I much believe in magic. I did not for an instant, for example, think yesterday's puddle quarter was the cab quarter of last month returned to me perhaps by air in Wilmington. No. Another friend, a reporter at the paper, makes lists, with numbers, of what he has to do that day and even what he wants to talk to me about. He once sent me a letter from Chicago with the P.S. "What is your zip-code number, please?" He travels often. There they sit, though, the people who are so free and easy with their disapproval, at their table in the restaurant, crunching the little bones.

Many English girls one meets abroad are called Vanessa. When a Van, or a Ness, in New York shut the cab door on her thumb, Sam called me from the emergency ward of the hospital. He had taken me home. He had dropped off Nessa next. Then she slammed the door that way, and he took her to the hospital. It was two A.M. He called me because he thought it might help to have a woman around. I put on jeans and a shirt. I took some Scotch along. The emergency ward was full of the slightly injured, mainly knife wounds at that hour, and Sam. Nessa was having her thumb set. We of the emergency ward passed around the Scotch. When Nessa came out, with the intern who had put a cast on her thumb and wrist, it was 3:15. On the way out of the hospital, I thought I was going to faint. Then, I thought how unseemly it would be to have to be carried back into the hospital. I think you are not altogether American unless you have been to Mississippi; you are not a patriot if you start to faint when somebody breaks her thumb. Anyway, I never faint.

Most of the cars that tried to run us down were off-duty cabs. Sam finally found a cab to take Nessa home. On account of her thumb, she needed help with her keys, so we walked her to the door. As Sam put the key in the lock, her mother-in-law stood there, distraught. She looked at Sam, with his rimless glasses and his beard, and at me in my shirt and jeans. She screamed. Then she started to cry. She looked at Nessa. "I knew it," she said. "What have they done to you?"

Last night at dinner, a man said that, on principle, he never answers his telephone. Somebody asked him how he reached people. "I call them," he said. "But suppose they don't believe in answering, either?" I thought of phones ringing all over New York, no one answering. Like people bringing themselves off in every single adjoining co-op of a luxury building. Or the streets entirely cleared of traffic, except ambulances. We spoke of a friend of ours who had died the night before, at forty-three. "But my God! I'm forty-one," a bearded banker said. "Don't worry," his wife, who is German, answered. "There is no order. It is not a line." I often meet people who do not like me or each other. It doesn't always matter. I keep on smiling, talking. I knock at the same door once, three times, twelve. My dislike has no consequences. It accrues only in my mind—like preserves on a shelf or guns zeroing in, and never firing. The same smile. I knew someone who used to go to sleep counting, not sheep, but people against whom he had grievances—bullies from childhood, kindergarten teachers, back to nannies even, bosses, employees, anybody awful up to the preceding day. When they were rounded up in his mind, he would machine-gun them down. If it turned out he had left out anybody, he would have to start all over. Round them up. Gun them down again. Slept without difficulty. Judgment Day may be compiled of private arsenals like these.

Four-leaf clovers. I have one that somebody who always finds them gave me and one I found myself. Many children take a stem from one three-leaf clover and a stem and a leaf from another and tie the stems together, in full consciousness that it is not the same. I know that. When I was last at my wit's end, I dreamed I parked my car on my way to my stabled horse and found the country roadside absolutely

35

strewn with silver. It was also overgrown with poison ivy, vicious, three-leafed, shining. It was by no means a parable about capitalism and making money. I believe in both, and would not think of dreaming against either. Anyway, I do not dream in parables.

But poison ivy. Many people, particularly children, have had poison ivy very often, very badly. They speak of it. They do not forget it. But there is an outer limit, a kind that passes any question of degree. Those who have utterly had it instantly recognize each other—like the Jews and homosexuals in Proust. It has no dignity whatever. There are no poison-ivy heroes. As homesickness, at camp or school, can be a first intuition of death and bereavement, this creeping thing is most nearly a child's premonitory sense of mortal illness. I had it once when I needed to be led blindly to the school infirmary by a girl who had the flu. I put two fingers around her wrist so she could lead me. The next day there was a neat circle of poison ivy around her wrist. That was a friend. There are other such cabals, reverse elites of outer limit, junkies, sufferers from migraines, the truly seasick, soldiers' fear in wartime, certain cramps. Many people suffer from cramps severely, turn quite silent, green, and shaky. Someone offers them a glass of gin. But there are cramps of an entirely other order, when even hardened doctors—knowing it is not important, only temporary, just a matter of hours—reach for the Demerol and the needle. It must be so in each lonely degrading thing from which one comes back having learned nothing whatever. There are no conclusions to be drawn from it. Lonely people see double entendres everywhere.

There are times when every act, no matter how private or unconscious, becomes political. Whom you live with, how you wear your hair, whether you marry, whether you insist that your child take piano lessons, what are the brand names on your shelf; all these become political decisions. At other times, no act—no campaign or tract, statement or rampage

—has any political charge at all. People with the least sense of which times are, and which are not, political are usually most avid about politics. At six one morning, Will went out in jeans and frayed sweater to buy a quart of milk. A tourist bus went by. The megaphone was directed at him. "There's one," it said. That was in the 1960's. Ever since, he's wondered. There's one what?

In covering fires, murders, blasts, quotidian disasters, raffle winners, just walking through the streets, like everyone, I often meet a beggar. I always, always give a quarter or a dime. In recent years, always. I once met a girl called Yael in Beersheba, very poor, who always did, without reflection—gave a little something to each beggar, even ones she passed twice, even the most devastated. She did not look around to see who noticed, simply gave. Now every tin cup —with or without pencils, voice, accordion—stops me. It is not a bribe to my own fortunes any longer. Even lighting candles in a church, I have never prayed quite in specifics. It is just a habit now.

"Forget it," says the drunken voice outside. "What's it for? Throw it away."

My life began, really, at college, where I nearly always slept. Waking, I studied—clinical psychology. We ran rats in mazes by the hour, checking whether rats rewarded learned things faster. At the end of half the mazes, the cheese stood alone. We also ran tests on each other—lie detectors, free-word associations with a stopwatch; the point turned out to be not what you said but just how long you stalled before you said it. Weekends, I took trains. You never knew whom you might meet. There was a man who peddled cigars, cigarettes, and what he pronounced "magazynes" outside the Philadelphia station, and a dining-car waiter who offered you among other cheeses, "camemberry." I never did meet anyone.

I was going to be a doctor and an analyst, but in my third year an odd thing happened. There was a group of friends by this time, an improbable, warm set of debutantes and scholars—girls who liked each other, dated each other's brothers, cousins. I belonged. One night, climbing a brick wall to the dorm long after hours, I got poison ivy. Totally. Again. Those ivy-covered walls. My case, however, was diagnosed as an allergy to something in the chemistry laboratory. I knew just what I did have, but I didn't argue long. My work had started to be awful. I allowed myself to be persuaded just to drop it. After graduation, we were all many times each other's bridesmaids. The marriages were in Maryland, Boston, New Hampshire, California, Georgia, Maine.

Just south of the Mason-Dixon line, on several weekends, young men—clean-cut, friendly, slightly tipsy—from Princeton or the University of Virginia Law School would rise late in the evening and propose a toast to the N.L.A. We all drank to it. I finally asked, and learned it was the Nigger Lynching Association. My friends from those days have changed as much as all the world has. We are still friends. In those days, too, there was the matter of religion, which tended both to start and to inhibit conversation. Once, the father of my roommate asked me whether I had gone to the same boarding school as his daughter. I said no. There was a pause. He asked me how long I had known her. I said a year. There was another pause. Finally, he made another try. "Do you," he asked, "know Eddie Warburg?" But it turned out all right. Another bridesmaid, this one from Alabama, had brought an Argentine boyfriend from the Catholic University in Washington. He was very rich, with more profound good manners than any Anglo-Saxon I have met, but he had not troubled much with haircuts. After we had all swum awhile outside, the bride's mother asked me in confidential tones whether I thought she ought to drain the pool.

"Well, you know, you can't win them all," the old bartender said. "In fact, you can't win any of them."

Lyda was an exuberant, even a dramatic gardener. She would spend hours in her straw hat and gloves, bending over the soil. When somebody walked past her in her work, she was always holding up a lettuce or a bunch of radishes, with an air of resolute courage, as though she had shot them herself.

Will and I once went for a few days to the Caribbean, where we chartered what was called a yacht. He is married to his work, but there we were. Most of the boats had been rented by people from Chicago or Milwaukee. They were bossed around by the crews and owners. They wore strange shirts and shorts and drank a lot of rum. Our boat, however, was a question of expediency. We wanted to get as quickly as possible to an island which had no airfield. The boat was run by three Swiss—Hans the father, Hans the son, and the mother, Trude, I think, or Hannelore. We tried to find out, in our few hours, why three Swiss happened to be running a yacht in the Caribbean. It turned out that Hans the father had owned a gas station in Geneva. He had sailed, with his family, on the lake there. Then he bought a larger boat and tried the Atlantic. They barely made it. Hans sold the boat in Florida. They went back to Geneva. The family started feeling landlocked. They bought another boat from their profits on the first one, crossed the sea again, and began doing charters. They were not like the lounging, bossy owners. They were still, in fact, scandalized by their last charter—a priest and what he said were his two sisters. It was not the more obvious situation that appalled them. It was that, their boat having no refrigerator, the wife of Hans the father kept the vegetables in the bathtub. The priest, without removing even the lettuce, had taken his showers in that tub, over what was going to be half of dinner. They could not get over this. They thought of selling their boat again and returning to Geneva. The jet, the telephone, the boat, the train, the television. Dislocations.

The radical intelligence in the moderate position is the only place where the center holds. Or so it seems.

My new life has its contrasts. One weekend, I was sent to cover a hospital in Brooklyn—municipal, enormous, patients mostly black. My subject was the emergency ward on weekends, but a middle-aged black doctor, graduate of Howard in the thirties, took me on a tour. The wards were jammed —diseases, fractures, burns. The severely burned had a little ward room of their own because they so depress the other patients. Wounded criminal suspects had semiprivate rooms with police outside them. These were luxury accommodations. All patients—even those about to "slip away," in the doctor's euphemism—were silent, except one white lady who screamed occasionally from senile psychosis. It was as though the entire place were drugged.

One lady patient, very ill, had been put in the corridor, her bed alongside the wall, blocking the water cooler. Every intern and nurse, rushing harassed and anxious down that hall, would absent-mindedly pull the bed aside along its casters, take a drink of water, slam the bed against the wall again. All else was silent. I thought I'd had my tour when the doctor, returning to his office, noticed a silhouette through his glass-panelled door. "Oh," he said. "This will interest you. You mustn't miss this." Then he told the young black man waiting in the office that his sister was about to slip away. We went down the ward to see the sister. I was introduced and said, "How are you?" She said, "Fine thanks. How are you?"

Toward early morning, activity in the emergency ward accelerated, a catastrophe a minute, mostly victims of knife fights whom other hospitals—uneasy with police cases—had simply passed along. Two interns were Hungarian refugees who had had full practices in Budapest, two were young Egyptians, all were gray with tiredness. A case arrived upon a stretcher. Two policemen asked routinely who had cut him. He said he did not know. Two hours later, still waiting for an operating room for him to become empty, the cut man's wife saw a young man enter at the far end of the room. She said quite softly to an intern, "That's him. That's the man that did it." The intern called a policeman.

The wife told of her husband's being held against a tub in the hall bathroom of their building and cut, for reasons she could not explain. The young man himself had come in to have a knife wound on his right palm treated. When confronted with the story, and the evidence of his own wounded hand, the accused young man denied it. The police brought him to the man upon the stretcher. He leaned solicitously over the weak man and said, "I didn't do it, did I? Tell them." The weak man looked up and said, "Yeah, man. You did. You cut me." Then he shut his eyes. They wheeled him to the operating room to fix him up.

I am not technically a Catholic. That is, I have not informed or asked the Church. I do not, certainly, believe in evolution. For example, fossils. I believe there are objects in nature—namely, fossils—which occur in layers, and which some half-rational fantasts insist derive from animals, the bottom ones more ancient than the top. The same, I think, with word derivations—arguments straining back to Sanskrit or Indo-European. I have never seen a word derive. It seems to me that there are given things, all strewn and simultaneous. Even footprints, except in detective stories, now leave me in some doubt that anyone passed by. People who are less happy, I find, are always consoling those who are more. At table, there are often one or two people who stammer. The well-bred stammer that pretends the speaker is not quite firm in what he's stated, is still open to suggestion—open mind. And the real stammer that bears down so hard on language that it seems absolute, a way to occupy airwaves, until the speaker has quite formulated his transmission. I have noticed that stammerers talk a lot. The chaplain, though, who was the best interpreter in the history of the monastery at the border, had a violent speech disorder in his native tongue.

We had been standing outside his tent for eleven hours. The crowd was large. When at last he came out, the guru stared, then threw an orange, savagely. He returned to his tent. That was all.

The other night, I interviewed a controversial diplomat, an ex- and future politician with strong ideas on air pollution. He took me home. By the time I had answered the telephone ringing in my bedroom, he had started an enormous fire in the fireplace of my living room. I only have two rooms, kitchen, and bath. He had taken off his jacket, fixed himself and me a drink, and sat upon the sofa. He was so good at all this that for the first time in months I felt at home. For an hour and a half, I did not tell him that I had a deadline. By that time, the fire was blazing firmly and correctly. The diplomat had been a country boy. When I finally did mention my deadline at the office, he looked surprised, then said good-naturedly the brownstone would catch fire if we left the fireplace in flames. It was quite true. I asked him how to put it out. He said, "Sand, baby." I have no sand in my apartment. We poured water from every pan and kettle in the kitchen. It took some time. We also drenched the carpet. When I woke up at noon the next day, the wet wood and ashes with a kettle still beside them looked like some desolate form of art.

In Paris, where I studied anthropology (the structural, not field work), some American anthropologists on Fulbrights gave a party for some Africans, in my apartment. The Africans were all students at the École Normale Superieure. They might one day all be prime ministers. A student from the Ivory Coast said he had as many names as the midwife could reel off in the moments when he was actually being born. The daughter of a former British high commissioner in

Nigeria danced the high life with a student from the Belgian Congo. A small, blond French-Canadian girl left the party early, to go to bed with one of the Americans. She asked him later when they would see each other again. He said, "Don't break the magic." Afterward, he left for Mali. Most people left the party very late. It was a year when it was rumored that *Life* was going to do an article on American expatriates in Paris. Perhaps there is that rumor every year or two. In any case, the Americans stopped washing their hair, wrote poetry, and were seen much in cafés, complaining of publicity. At the party, though, they stayed so long I left and took a room in a hotel.

The doctor we all loved in high school set fractures at the foot of the ski slope. He also worked part-time at the prison. Except for a spectacular, unsolved murder in the forties, committed by someone we all knew, the prison is the thing for which our town is known. It used to be known for its main street—which was an infuriating obstacle to traffic between New York and Boston. But now there is a highway. The prison is important. We have had every major federal offender anyone can remember—corrupt, embezzling politicians while they were being re-elected, conscientious objectors, all sorts of federal offenders, radical clergy, spies. The prison baseball team plays with teams from the local stores and factories. On sports pages, the prison line-ups differ from those of local teams only by the omission of last names. Tom J., from the prison, for example, pitched, and so on. Anyway, the doctor we all loved in high school went on from setting fractures to a flirtation with homeopathy. He could not bear suffering. When patients called to say they had colds, he would whistle and say God, I can hear it. When they had sprained ankles, he would inhale and say that he knew how it hurt, he had had sprains himself. Homeopathy failed him. He became a great internist, orthodox, modern. Then, he went to Tennessee, and found himself faced with victims of hexes. They were in comas. They seemed to be dying. He tried orthodox medicine. They got worse. He got angry. Then he gave in. He started circling their beds three times, with lighted candles. That was the accepted practice in the region, and it worked.

I have often been in hotels alone. It is no good unless you're on assignment. One sits in the lobby, the bar, or worst of all the restaurant, with a book, and pretends to be preoccupied. One gets soup or vegetables on the pages, and they stick. One summer, in Malta, I took a book from my hotel room to the beach. The beach was full of English tourists, grocers already tanned from fingertips to wrist, from hair to collar line, standing in bathing suits and shoes and socks, with arms folded across their chests, staring out to sea. Also blond divorcées, deeply brown, lying in beach chairs, with a transistor and perhaps one small weedy child digging in wet and littered sand. At the post office, there was an enormous lady with a considerable mustache, who took grave pleasure in slavering on all the stamps whenever anyone brought in a letter. I took off for a smaller island, Gozo, which was quieter. There was a sign quite near the water: CAUTION. DO NOT TOUCH OR PICK UP STRANGE OBJECTS FOUND ON THE BEACH. REPORT THEM IMMEDIATELY TO THE POLICE. Mines. Malta and Gozo had a rough time in the war.

Our obituary writer is an extreme, pedantic gossip. He gets things wrong, but he gets them in detail. I had just started working at the paper. He thought I was an alcoholic; he told it to a man on night rewrite, who told it to all the people in the newsroom, who told it to the people at the culture desk. It is not so troubling to be thought an alcoholic; still, I preferred not. When he asked me out to lunch, I gladly went. His parents are from Poland. His name is Standish Hawthorne Smith. We went to a Greek restaurant. When we sat down, he held my hand. He asked me whether Will has his divorce. I did not know quite what to say. I asked about his work. He smiled. He asked what I would like to drink.

Nothing, I thought. Then I remembered that nothing would be the order of an alcoholic on the wagon. My normal Scotch and water would not do. I asked for an ouzo. No alcoholic in his right mind, I thought, would have an ouzo. I had two. Standish walked me home. He said he wrote, and read, a lot of poetry. When we got to my door, he asked whether he might use the phone. He made three phone calls, going to the kitchen now and then, to pour himself another vodka. I sat in the living room, with a glass of wine. I had altogether lost my sense of purpose in the situation. After his hour or two of phone calls, he came to the living room. "Do you know," he said, "three things are said to be true of every Polish houseguest. First, he raids your icebox. Then he reads your mail. Then he fires the maid." He walked to a window, pulled the curtains, asked whether I would like him to fire the maid. He finally read some poetry instead. Anyway, Will's gone.

I used to live with a graduate student of political science, a kind of Calvinist in reverse; that is, he was uncompromisingly bohemian. His mother was a dancer. His father was a judge. Our mattress was on the floor. We had no lights or telephone. Each morning when he left, I cooked a meal according to a recipe, most carefully, then tasted it and found it good, and threw it out. A trial run. In two hours, he would be back from the library. We would have beer, two sandwiches, perhaps a nap. Then he would go back to the library. All afternoon, I would cook the meal again, with better confidence, studying the cookbook with the concentration I still had from graduate school. It would be supper this time, practiced, complicated, natural—after cigarettes and gin, which we drank neat.

He had an intimation, a skepticism of all this domesticity. It seemed to me one of the minor deceptions, though most fraught. My friends, after all, were married—to men whose hours were already set. Adam might come home from his books or his little office at the university at any time. The food waste would have appalled him, the deception even more. He lived on frankness and economy. He wrote sometimes: "The first sentence can be like the rapping of a gavel, or it can sidle up to endear itself. It can thump you on the back with fraternal heartiness, or it can tap you for a loan. There are writers like prosecutors, and others with a bedside manner, and others still, with that particular note of instruction which can drive you up the wall. The thing is, I recognize every literary style at once, and I detest them all." So on. I was trying translations of some sort of diaries. "An appointment is less romantic than a rendezvous. A rendezvous is more clandestine than a date. How to explain, then, that I saw my lover yesterday, that he is a prince, an assassin, a masterspy. And also my immediate boss. No, no." I simply could not cook. Logic seemed to require those trial runs in the kitchen, which were entirely alien to his cast of mind, entirely natural to mine. I was prepared to go to lengths. I guess I overdid it. My sense of limit in these things was shot. I got a job reporting. Then we left each other. Here I am.

In the first year, the *Standard* sent me to those poor sensational families, until they had become so commonplace they were no longer news but subject for political reflection by our feature writers. Anyway, there was the Movement in the South. Then, there were demonstrations against so many things. I went to a meeting of black school principals in Anacostia, Washington, D.C. I went as a reporter and Consultant. A consultant. By that time, any journalist who had stuck a while with unsensational blacks was accepted as of their number in that way.

At lunch the first day in the cafeteria of the University of Maryland, where the conference was, a one-armed black teacher asked me to cut his meat. I have the shakes a good part of the time (which interferes no end with taking notes). I tried to cut his ham steak. I was shaking quite a lot. I think he thought it was because of his lost arm. He said, "Sweetheart, you need a drink." That part of Maryland is dry. He offered me the key to his room, in which he had a fifth of bourbon. The number on his room key was the same as mine. It turned out that by some bureaucratic mix-up at least four people had the same single-room assignment—two ministers, the teacher, and I. We all found rooms elsewhere. I called old friends in Bethesda.

When the meetings were over, around midnight, there were of course no cabs. A small, kind black Anacostia parent, owner of a funeral parlor, offered to drive me to Bethesda—which he graciously said was only twenty minutes out of his own way home. Two hours later, we were still driving. I thought he was lost. Then I thought he wasn't. Suddenly, he pulled over to the side of the highway. I thought, Good grief, I am over twenty. I am a liberal. I should have thought it through. But does it need to be right here beside four lanes of nighttime traffic? A white state trooper had pulled up behind us. The Anacostia parent turned off the ignition. "We've done something wrong, I guess," he said. I thought, But we haven't. The trooper shined his flashlight through the windshield. He said, "Folks, you made a wrong turn at that last turnoff. Lots of people miss it." We drove on to Bethesda. The Anacostia parent had been truly lost.

In his small, airless apartment the sportswriter served local wine, cheap Scotch, and beer. His wife, and the other sportswriters' wives, four of them pregnant, two not apparently so, sat in the bedroom, drinking the Almadén, with ice. They discussed rents. The sportswriters, hitting the Scotch and the beer, sat in the living room, talking of books they planned to write but never would. The pressures were wrong. There was just enough money and not enough time. No one was rich. No one was poor. No one was ever going to do anything of any consequence. We were talking about *No, No, Nanette.* I said I thought there was such a thing as an Angry Bravo—that those audiences who stand, and cheer, and roar, and seem altogether beside themselves at what they would instantly agree is at best an unimportant thing, are not really cheering *No, No, Nanette.* They are booing *Hair.* Or whatever else it is on stage that they hate and that seems to triumph. So they stand and roar. Every bravo is not so much a Yes to the frail occasion they have come to make a stand at, as a No, goddam it to everything else, a bravo of rage. And with that, they become, for what it's worth, a constituency that is political. When they find each other, and stand and roar like that, they want, they want to be reckoned with.

Joe said, Isn't it possible they just want to say that they are having a good time? It's possible; one ought perhaps to take into account that it is fun to be part of an audience that wants to roar. Norma asked whether Joe had seen it. He said no. Norma said, "Well, then you don't know. It's not a musical audience roar. It's not an avant garde roar. It's a march roar. A rally roar. A parade roar." Joe said, "You mean a lynch roar." Norma said, "Now that's going too far."

Just two nights ago, I went to a party with three large dinner tables. It was mixed, the rich and famous and the reporters who had helped them on their way. There were some intellectual sharks, some arrivistes, some sheep, good souls, professors, editors, some radicals, who themselves invite poets, novelists, sophomore rioters, and visiting Englishmen to dinner, which is served by maids. This party was given by two kind, intelligent Americans I knew from college. They wanted to do good and to *know,* like people out of E. M. Forster or Henry James. The purpose was for the senior senator of an American liberal state and an Indian dignitary, a woman, to meet a cross section of American opinion. They met it. The first course was aspic. The dignitary thought somebody was going to attack her for Indian educational policies in Kerala. No one knew anything about India at all. She relaxed and grew bored. The senator thought he was going to meet the young and learn about them. I was sitting next to him. I said I thought he and I might be among the last three people in the room who still believed in the electoral process. He said, "Thanks, sweetheart."

Suddenly, after dessert, a lady at my table—a donor to controversial social causes, now half persuaded to devote her money to the cause of saving art—said she thought the dinner would be wasted if the conversation did not become general, if it was all private bon mots spliced together, or just gossip. She thought we ought to talk about America today. She called first on one of those social academics, a man who had *vecu* a bit, whose bow tie was perpetually atilt, perhaps to show himself at an eccentric angle to the dinner jackets that he wore, what they implied. He rose, red-faced and angry, to his feet. He said he felt this country now was the world's most murderous and corrupt. He happened to know, he said, of two deaths at Kent State that had not been reported, and of other grave matters he was not at liberty to disclose. He felt the only hope for humanity now lay in the vitality and idealism of the third world.

The lady who led the discussion, unperturbed, asked a tireless, self-effacing worker in the cause of civil rights whether he had anything to say "about all this." He leaned his head against the wall, then stood up. "Bertram," he said, "I am so offended by what you have just said, I don't know what to say to you." He sat down. The lady called upon a poet, a surrealist who, with clear reluctance, got to his feet and said, turning to the Indian lady, "I think in this country we need to disburden ourselves of our, our burden of rationality." He sat down. It did not seem exactly India's problem.

A liberal reporter of military affairs was called on. He said he didn't want to discuss the morality of it, but that anyone who had covered the military would know . . . ; "I know something about the military," another reporter, younger, fiercer, gray with anger, said, rising to his feet and interrupting. Then he said he knew that the fabric of our whole society was stretching very thin. The editors—one local popular, one national radical—talked well when they were called on, discursive, rambling. It was as though they had a repressed and abiding wish to have their say, in their own words for once.

49

The party ended the only way it could. A McLuhanite apostle, revered as a physics genius in these circles, spoke. He was in his seventies, extremely hard of hearing. He spoke long and loudly. He continued speaking. "I'm sorry to have to interrupt," the lady moderator said, after geologic time spans passed. He did not hear her. He went on.

"I'm very sorry to have to interrupt," she said, more loudly. He heard nothing. He continued speaking. She kept trying. Finally, some clear-sighted soul rose to propose a toast. "All stand," he said. Everyone stood. For a few moments the clear-sighted soul and the deaf genius were speaking in duet. Then the genius, looking around, subsided. "The reason we are gathered here is to honor our hostess," the good soul said, and drained his glass. So did we all, and then went home with all deliberate speed. I took a cab home. The driver ranted. We passed three men, two beating up a third. They had pulled his sweatshirt up over his eyes. He could not see them. A crowd had gathered, interested. Suddenly a young man got out of the cab beside mine. "That's enough!" he shouted. The scene froze a minute. Then it started up again. After all, he was unarmed; nobody knew him. He moved closer. He said, "That's enough," again. The whole thing stopped, dissolved. The beaten man pulled his sweatshirt down over his injured face, put his arms inside the sleeves, and limped away. The crowd disintegrated. I thought, What a phrase from some past time I can remember. That's enough.

In the South, in simpler days, I remember a middle-aged gentle black worker speaking to his son who had insomnia. "When you can't sleep," he said, "just tell yourself the story of your life." Now sometimes when I can't sleep, I wonder. A twenty-four-hour curfew every day, for everybody. Suppose we blow up the whole thing. Everything. Everybody. Me. Buildings. No room. Blast. All dead. No survivors. And then I would say, and then I would say, Let's just have it a little quiet around here.

BROWNSTONE

The camel, I had noticed, was passing, with great difficulty, through the eye of the needle. The Apollo flight, the four-minute mile, Venus in Scorpio, human records on land and at sea—these had been events of enormous importance. But the camel, practicing in near obscurity for almost two thousand years, was passing through. First the velvety nose, then the rest. Not many were aware. But if the lead camel and then perhaps the entire caravan could make it, the thread, the living thread of camels, would exist, could not be lost. No one could lose the thread. The prospects of the rich would be enhanced. "Ortega tells us that the business of philosophy," the professor was telling his class of indifferent freshmen, "is to crack open metaphors which are dead."

"I shouldn't have come," the Englishman said, waving his drink and breathing so heavily at me that I could feel my bangs shift. "I have a terrible cold."

"He would probably have married her," a voice across the room said, "with the exception that he died."

"Well, I am a personality that prefers not to be annoyed."

"We should all prepare ourselves for this eventuality."

A six-year-old was passing the hors d'oeuvres. The baby, not quite steady on his feet, was hurtling about the room.

"He's following me," the six-year-old said, in despair.

"Then lock yourself in the bathroom, dear," Inez replied.

"He always waits outside the door."

"He loves you, dear."

"Well, I don't like it."

"How I envy you," the minister's wife was saying to a courteous, bearded boy, "reading *Magic Mountain* for the first time."

The homosexual across the hall from me always takes Valium and walks his beagle. I borrow Valium from him from time to time, and when he takes a holiday the dog is left with me. On our floor of this brownstone, we are friends. Our landlord, Roger Somerset, was murdered last July. He was a kind and absent-minded man, and on the night when he was stabbed there was a sort of requiem for him in the heating system. There is a lot of music in this building anyway. The newlyweds on the third floor play Bartók on their stereo. The couple on the second floor play clarinet quintets; their kids play rock. The girl on the fourth floor, who has been pining for two months, plays Judy Collins' "Maid of Constant Sorrow" all day long. We have a kind of orchestra in here. The ground floor is a shop. The owner of the shop speaks of our landlord's murder still. Shaking his head, he says that he suspects "foul play." We all agree with him. We

52

changed our locks. But "foul play" seems a weird expression for the case.

It is all weird. I am not always well. One block away (I often think of this), there was ten months ago an immense crash. Water mains broke. There were small rivers in the streets. In a great skyscraper that was being built, something had failed. The newspapers reported the next day that by some miracle only two people had been "slightly injured" by ten tons of falling steel. The steel fell from the eighteenth floor. The question that preoccupies me now is how, under the circumstances, slight injuries could occur. Perhaps the two people were grazed in passing by. Perhaps some fragments of the sidewalk ricocheted. I knew a deliverer of flowers who, at Sixty-ninth and Lexington, was hit by a flying suicide. Situations simply do not yield to the most likely structures of the mind. A "self-addressed envelope," if you are inclined to brood, raises deep questions of identity. Such an envelope, immutably itself, is always precisely where it belongs. "Self-pity" is just sadness, I think, in the pejorative. But "joking with nurses" fascinates me in the press. Whenever someone has been quite struck down, lost faculties, members of his family, he is said to have "joked with his nurses" quite a lot. What a mine of humor every nurse's life must be.

I have a job, of course. I have had several jobs. I've had our paper's gossip column since last month. It is egalitarian. I look for people who are quite obscure, and report who is breaking up with whom and where they go and what they wear. The person who invented this new form for us is on antidepressants now. He lives in Illinois. He says there are people in southern Illinois who have not yet been covered by the press. I often write about families in Queens. Last week, I went to a dinner party on Park Avenue. After 1 A.M., something called the Alive or Dead Game was being played.

53

Someone would mention an old character from Tammany or Hollywood. "Dead," "Dead," "Dead," everyone would guess. "No, no. Alive. I saw him walking down the street just yesterday," or "Yes. Dead. I read a little obituary notice about him last year." One of the little truths people can subtly enrage or reassure each other with is who—when you have looked away a month, a year—is still around.

The St. Bernard at the pound on Ninety-second Street was named Bonnie and would have cost five dollars. The attendant held her tightly on a leash of rope. "Hello, Bonnie," I said. Bonnie growled. "I wouldn't talk to her if I was you," the attendant said. I leaned forward to pat her ear. Bonnie snarled. "I wouldn't touch her if I was you," the attendant said. I held out my hand under Bonnie's jowls. She strained against the leash, and choked and coughed. "Now cut that out, Bonnie," the attendant said. "Could I just take her for a walk around the block," I said, "before I decide?" "Are you out of your mind?" the attendant said. Aldo patted Bonnie, and we left.

DEAR TENANT:

We have reason to believe that there are impostors posing as Con Ed repairmen and inspectors circulating in this area.

Do not permit any Con Ed man to enter your premises or the building, if possible.

THE PRECINCT

The New York Chinese cabdriver lingered at every corner and at every traffic light, to read his paper. I wondered what the news was. I looked over his shoulder. The illustrations and the type were clear enough: newspaper print, pornographic fiction. I leaned back in my seat. A taxi-driver who happened to be Oriental with a sadomasochistic cast of mind was not my business. I lit a cigarette, looked at my bracelet.

I caught the driver's eyes a moment in the rearview mirror. He picked up his paper. "I don't think you ought to read," I said, "while you are driving." Traffic was slow. I saw his mirrored eyes again. He stopped his reading. When we reached my address, I did not tip him. Racism and prudishness, I thought, and reading over people's shoulders.

But there are moments in this place when everything becomes a show of force. He can read what he likes at home. Tipping is still my option. Another newspaper event, in our brownstone. It was a holiday. The superintendent normally hauls the garbage down and sends the paper up, by dumbwaiter, each morning. On holidays, the garbage stays upstairs, the paper on the sidewalk. At 8 A.M., I went downstairs. A ragged man was lying across the little space that separates the inner door, which locks, from the outer door, which doesn't. I am not a news addict. I could have stepped over the sleeping man, picked up my *Times,* and gone upstairs to read it. Instead, I knocked absurdly from inside the door, and said, "Wake up. You'll have to leave now." He got up, lifted the flattened cardboard he had been sleeping on, and walked away, mumbling and reeking. It would have been kinder, certainly, to let the driver read, the wino sleep. One simply cannot bear down so hard on all these choices.

What is the point. That is what must be borne in mind. Sometimes the point is really who wants what. Sometimes the point is what is right or kind. Sometimes the point is a momentum, a fact, a quality, a voice, an intimation, a thing said or unsaid. Sometimes it's who's at fault, or what will happen if you do not move at once. The point changes and goes out. You cannot be forever watching for the point, or you lose the simplest thing: being a major character in your own life. But if you are, for any length of time, custodian of the point—in art, in court, in politics, in lives, in rooms—it turns out there are rear-guard actions everywhere. To see a thing clearly, and when your vision of it dims, or when it goes to someone else, if you have a gentle nature, keep your silence, that is lovely. Otherwise, now and then, a small foray is worthwhile. Just so that being always, complacently, thoroughly wrong does not become the safest position of them all. The point has never quite been entrusted to me.

My cousin, who was born on February 29th, became a veterinarian. Some years ago, when he was twenty-eight (seven, by our childhood birthday count), he was drafted, and sent to Malaysia. He spent most of his military service there, assigned to the zoo. He operated on one tiger, which, in the course of abdominal surgery, began to wake up and wag its tail. The anesthetist grabbed the tail, and injected more sodium pentothal. That tiger survived. But two flamingos, sent by the city of Miami to Kuala Lumpur as a token of good will, could not bear the trip or the climate and, in spite of my cousin's efforts, died. There was also a cobra— the largest anyone in Kuala Lumpur could remember having seen. An old man had brought it, in an immense sack, from somewhere in the countryside. The zoo director called my cousin at once, around dinnertime, to say that an unprecedented cobra had arrived. Something quite drastic, however, seemed wrong with its neck. My cousin, whom I have always admired—for his leap-year birthday, for his pilot's license, for his presence of mind—said that he would certainly examine the cobra in the morning but that the best thing for it after its long journey must be a good night's rest. By morning, the cobra was dead.

My cousin is well. The problem is this. Hardly anyone about whom I deeply care at all resembles anyone else I have ever met, or heard of, or read about in the literature. I know an Israeli general who, in 1967, retook the Mitla Pass but who, since his mandatory retirement from military service at fifty-five, has been trying to repopulate the Ark. He asked me, over breakfast at the Drake, whether I knew any owners of oryxes. Most of the vegetarian species he has collected have already multiplied enough, since he has found and cared for them, to be permitted to run wild. The carnivorous animals, though, must still be kept behind barbed wire—to keep them from stalking the rarer vegetarians. I know a group that studies Proust one Sunday afternoon a month, and an analyst, with that Exeter laugh (embittered mooing noises, and mirthless heaving of the shoulder blades), who has the most remarkable terrorist connections in the Middle East.

The conversation of *The Magic Mountain* and the unrequited love of six-year-olds occurred on Saturday, at brunch. "Bring someone new," Inez had said. "Not queer. Not married, maybe separated. John and I are breaking up." The invitation was not of a kind that I had heard before. Aldo, who lives with me between the times when he prefers to be alone, refused to come. He despises brunch. He detests Inez. I went, instead, with an editor who has been a distant, steady friend but who, ten years ago, when we first came to New York, had once put three condoms on the night table beside the phone. We both had strange ideas then about New York. Aldo is a gentle, orderly, soft-spoken man, slow to conclude. I try to be tidy when he is here, but I have often made his cigarettes, and once his manuscript, into the bed. Our paper's publisher is an intellectual from Baltimore. He has read Wittgenstein; he's always making unimpeachable remarks. Our music critic throws a tantrum every day, in print. Our book reviewer is looking for another job. He found that the packages in which all books are mailed could not, simply could not, be opened without doing considerable damage— through staples, tape, wire, fluttering gray stuff, recalcitrance —to the reviewer's hands. He felt it was a symptom of some kind—one of those cases where incompetence at every stage, across the board, acquired a certain independent force. Nothing to do with books, he thought, worked out at all. We also do the news. For horoscopes, there are the ladies' magazines, which tell you—earnestly—auspicious times to shave your legs. We just cannot compete.

"All babies are natural swimmers," John said, lowering his two-year-old son gently over the side of the rowboat, and smiling. The child thrashed and sank. Aldo dived in and grabbed him. The baby came up coughing, not crying, and looked with pure fear at his father. John looked with dismay at his son. "He would have come up in a minute," John said to Aldo, who was dripping and rowing. "You have to give nature a chance."

My late landlord was from Scarsdale. The Maid of Constant Sorrow is from Texas. Aldo is from St. Louis. Inez's versions vary about where she's from. I grew up in a New England mill town, where, in the early thirties, all the insured factories burned down. It has been difficult to get fire insurance in that region ever since. The owner of a hardware store, whose property adjoined an insured factory at the time, lost everything. Afterward, he walked all day along the railroad track, waiting for a train to run him down. Railroad service has never been very good up there. No trains came. His children own the town these days, for what it's worth. The two cobbled streets where black people always lived have been torn up and turned into a public park since a flood that occurred some years ago. Unprecedented rains came. Retailers had to destroy their sodden products, for fear of contamination. The black section was torn up and seeded over in the town's rezoning project. No one knows where the blacks live now. But there are Negroes in the stores and schools, and on the football team. It is assumed that the park integrated the town. Those black families must be living somewhere. It is a mystery.

At the women's college where I went, we had distinguished faculty in everything, digs at Nuoro and Mycenae. We had a quality of obsession in our studies. For professors who had quarreled with their wives at breakfast, those years of bright-eyed young women, never getting any older, must have been a trial. The head of the history department once sneezed into his best student's honors thesis. He slammed it shut. It was ultimately published. When I was there, a girl called Cindy Melchior was immensely fat. She wore silk trousers and gilt mules. One day, in the overheated classroom, she laid aside her knitting and lumbered to the window, which she opened. Then she lumbered back. "Do you think," the professor asked, "you are so graceful?" He somehow meant it kindly. Cindy wept. That year, Cindy's brother Melvin phoned me. "I would have called you sooner," he said, "but I had the most terrible eczema." All the service staff on campus in those days were black. Many of them were followers of Father Divine. They took new names in the church. I remember the year when a maid called Serious Heartbreak married a janitor called Universal Dictionary. At a meeting of the faculty last fall, the college president, who is new and male, spoke of raising money. A female professor of Greek was knitting—and working on Linear B, with an abacus before her. In our time, there was a vogue for madrigals. Some of us listened, constantly, to a single record. There was a phrase we could not decipher. A professor of symbolic logic, a French Canadian, had sounds that matched but a meaning that seemed unlikely: Sheep are no angels; come upstairs. A countertenor explained it, after a local concert: She'd for no angel's comfort stay. Correct, but not so likely either.

Paul: "Two diamonds."
Inez: "Two hearts."
Mary: "Three clubs."
John: "Four kings."
Inez: "Darling, you know you can't just bid four kings."
John: "I don't see why. I might have been bluffing."
Inez: "No, darling. That's poker. This is bridge. And even in poker you can't just bid four kings."
John: "No. Well, I guess we'd better deal another hand."

59

The host, for some reason, was taking Instamatic pictures of his guests. It was not clear whether he was doing this in order to be able to show, at some future time, that there had been this gathering in his house. Or whether he thought of pictures in some voodoo sense. Or whether he found it difficult to talk. Or whether he was bored. Two underground celebrities—one of whom had become a sensation by never generating or exhibiting a flicker of interest in anything, the other of whom was known mainly for hanging around the first—were taking pictures too. I was there with an actor I've known for years. He had already been received in an enormous embrace by an Eastern European poet, whose hair was cut too short but who was neither as awkwardly spontaneous nor as drunk as he cared to seem. The party was in honor of the poet, who celebrated the occasion by insulting everyone and being fawned upon, by distinguished and undistinguished writers alike. "This group looks as though someone had torn up a few guest lists and floated the pieces on the air," the actor said. The friend of the underground sensation walked up to us and said hello. Then, in a verbal seizure of some sort, he began muttering obscenities. The actor said a few calming things that didn't work. He finally put his finger on the mutterer's lips. The mutterer bit that finger extremely hard, and walked away. The actor wrapped his finger in a paper napkin, and got himself another drink. We stayed till twelve.

When I worked, for a time, in the infirmary of a branch of an upstate university, it was becoming more difficult with each passing semester, except in the most severe cases, to determine which students had mental or medical problems. At the clinic, young men with straggly beards and stained bluejeans wept alongside girls in jeans and frayed sweaters—all being fitted with contact lenses, over which they then wore granny glasses. There was no demand for prescription granny glasses at all. For the severely depressed, the para-noids, and the hallucinators, our young psychiatrists prescribed "mood elevators," pills that were neither uppers nor downers but which affected the bloodstream in such a way that within three to five weeks many sad outpatients became very cheerful, and several saints and historical figures became again Midwestern graduate students under tolerable stress. On one, not unusual, morning, the clinic had a call from an instructor in political science. "I am in the dean's office," he said. "My health is quite perfect. They want me to have a checkup."

"Oh?" said the doctor on duty. "Perhaps you could come in on Friday."

"The problem is," the voice on the phone said, "I have always thought myself, and been thought by others, a Negro. Now, through research, I have found that my family on both sides have always been white."

"Oh," the doctor on duty said. "Perhaps you could just take a cab and come over."

Within twenty minutes, the political-science instructor appeared at the clinic. He was black. The doctor said nothing, and began a physical examination. By the time his blood pressure was taken, the patient confided that his white ancestors were, in fact, royal. The mood elevators restored him. He and the doctor became close friends besides. A few months later, the instructor took a job with the government in Washington. Two weeks after that, he was calling the clinic again. "I have found new documentation," he said. "All eight of my great-grandparents were pure-blooded Germans—seven from Prussia, one from Alsace. I thought I should tell you, dear friend." The doctor suggested he come for the weekend. By Sunday afternoon, a higher dose of the pill had had its effect. The problem has not since recurred.

The Maid of Constant Sorrow said our landlord's murder marked a turning point in her analysis. "I don't feel guilty. I feel hated," she said. It is true, for a time, we all wanted to feel somehow part—if only because violence offset the ineluctable in our lives. My grandfather said that some people have such extreme insomnia that they look at their watches every hour after midnight, to see how sorry they ought to be feeling for themselves. Aldo says he does not care what my grandfather said. My grandmother refused to concede that any member of the family died of natural causes. An uncle's cancer in middle age occurred because all the suitcases fell off the luggage rack onto him when he was in his teens, and so forth. Death was an acquired characteristic. My grandmother, too, used to put other people's ailments into the diminutive: strokelets were what her friends had. Aldo said he was bored to tearsies by my grandmother's diminutives.

The weather last Friday was terrible. The flight to Martha's Vineyard was "decisional."

"What does 'decisional' mean?" a small boy asked. "It means we might have to land in Hyannis," his mother said. It is hard to understand how anyone learns anything.

Scattered through the two cars of the Brewster–New York train last week were adults with what seemed to be a clandestine understanding. They did not look at each other. They stared out the windows. They read. "Um," sang a lady at our fourth stop on the way to Grand Central. She appeared to be reading the paper. She kept singing her "Um," as one who is getting the pitch. A young man had already been whistling "Frère Jacques" for three stops. When the "Um" lady found her pitch and began to sing the national anthem, he looked at her with rage. The conductor passed through, punching tickets in his usual fashion, not in the aisle but directly over people's laps. Every single passenger was obliged to flick the tiny punched part of the ticket from his lap onto the floor. Conductors have this process as their own little show of force. The whistler and the singer were in a dead heat when we reached the city. The people with the clandestine understanding turned out to be inmates from somewhere upstate, now on leave with their families, who met them in New York.

I don't think much of writers in whom nothing is at risk. It is possible, though, to be too literal-minded about this question. In a magazine, under the heading "$3,000 for First-Person Articles," for example: "An article for this series must be a true, hitherto unpublished narrative of an unusual personal experience. It may be dramatic, inspirational, or humorous, but it must have, in the opinion of the editors, a quality of narrative interest comparable to 'How I Lost My Eye' (June '72) and 'Attacked by a Killer Shark' (April '72). Contributions must be typewritten, preferably *double-spaced* . . ." I particularly like where the stress, the italics, goes.

When the nanny drowned in the swimming pool, the parents reacted sensibly. They had not been there for the event. They had left the nanny at poolside with their youngest child, a girl of five, and the neighbor's twins, a boy and a girl of five, and the neighbor's baby-sitter, an *au pair*, who had become the nanny's dearest friend. When they returned from their morning round of golf, they found a fire truck in the yard, the drowned body of the nanny on the tiles, the three children playing, apparently calmly, under a tree, and two disconsolate firemen trying to deal with the neighbor's baby-sitter, who was hysterical. As an ambulance pulled into the driveway, the mother was already telephoning a doctor; her husband was giving the baby-sitter a glass of water and a sedative. When her hysterics had subsided, the baby-sitter explained what she could. Neither she nor the nanny, it turned out, could really swim. They could both manage a few strokes of the breaststroke, but they had a great fear of water over their heads. All three of what she called the "little ones" were strong and intrepid dog-paddlers. She and the nanny had always confined themselves to admonitions, and their own few stroking motions, from the shallow end. It was on account of these stroking motions that their inability really to swim had never come to anyone's attention or, for that matter, to their own. That morning, the nanny had, unaccountably, stroked a few feet out of her depth, in the direction of her charge. Then, according to the baby-sitter, who may have confused the sequence, things happened very rapidly, in the following order. Nanny's face turned blue. *Then* she swallowed water. Coughing and struggling, she reached her charge and clung to her. They both went under. Long seconds later, the little girl came up, crying and sputtering. In clear view, a few feet beyond the shallow end and beyond the grasp of the baby-sitter, who was trying to maintain her feet and her depth as she held out her hands, the nanny surfaced briefly once more, sank, and drowned.

I once met a polo-playing Argentine existential psychiatrist, who had lived for months in a London commune. He said that on days when the ordinary neurotics in the commune were getting on each other's nerves the few psychopaths and schizophrenics in their midst retired to their rooms and went their version of berserk, alone. On days when the neurotics got along, the psychopaths calmed down, tried to make contact, cooked. It was, he said, as though the sun came out for them. I hope that's true. Although altogether too much of life is mood. Aldo has a married friend who was in love for years with someone, also married. Her husband found out. He insisted that there be no more calls or letters. Aldo's friend called several times, reaching the husband. The girl herself would never answer. In the end, Aldo's friend—in what we regard as not his noblest gesture—sent all the girl's letters, addressed in a packet, to her husband. There was nothing more. I wonder whether the husband read those letters. If he did, I suppose he may have been a writer. In some sense. If not, he was a gentleman. There are also, on the bus, quite often ritual dancers, near-spastics who release the strap and begin a weird sequence of movements, always punctual, always the same. There are some days when everyone I see is lunatic.

I love the laconic. Clearly, I am not of their number. When animated conversations are going on, even with people interrupting one another, I have to curb an impulse to field every remark, by everybody, as though it were addressed to me. I have noticed this impulse in other people. It electrifies the room. It is resolved, sometimes, by conversations in a foreign language. One thinks, it is my turn to try to say something, to make an effort. One polishes a case, a tense, a comment. The subject passes. Just as well. There are, however, people who just sit there, silent. A question is addressed to them. They do not answer. Another question. Silence. It is a position of great power. Talkative people running toward those silences are jarred, time after time, by a straight arm rebuff. A quizzical look, a beautiful face perhaps, but silence. Everyone is exhausted, drinks too much, snarls later at home, wonders about the need for aspirin. It has been that stubborn wall.

I receive communications almost every day from an institution called the Center for Short-Lived Phenomena. Reporting sources all over the world, and an extensive correspondence. Under the title "Type of Event: Biological," I have received postcards about the progress of the Dormouse Invasion of Formentera: "Apart from population density, the dormouse of Formentera had a peak of reproduction in 1970. All females checked were pregnant, and perhaps this fact could have been the source of the idea of an 'invasion.' " And the Northwest Atlantic Puffin Decline. I have followed the Tanzanian Army Worm Outbreak. The San Fernando Earthquake. The Green Pond Fish Kill ("Eighty percent of the numbers involved," the Center's postcard reports, "were mummichogs.") The Samar Spontaneous Oil Burn. The Hawaiian Monk Seal Disappearance. And also, the Naini Tal Sudden Sky Brightening.

65

Those are accounts of things that did not last long, but if you become famous for a single thing in this country, and just endure, it is certain you will recur, enlarged. Of the eighteen men who were indicted for conspiracy to murder Schwerner, Goodman, and Chaney, seven were convicted by a Mississippi jury—a surprising thing. But then a year later, a man was wounded and a woman killed in a shootout while trying to bomb the house of some Mississippi Jews. It turned out that the informer, the man who had helped the bombers, and led the F.B.I. to them, was one of the convicted seven —the one, in fact, who was alleged to have killed two of the three boys who were found in that Mississippi dam. And what's more, and what's more, the convicted conspirator, alleged double killer, was paid thirty-six thousand dollars by the F.B.I. for bringing the bombers in. Yet the wave of anti-Semitic bombings in Mississippi stopped after the shoot-out. I don't know what it means. I am in this brownstone.

Last year, Aldo moved out and went to Los Angeles on a story. I called him to ask whether I could come. He said, "Are you going to stay this time?" I said I wasn't sure. I flew out quite early in the morning. On the plane, there was the most banal, unendurable pickup, lasting the whole flight. A young man and a young woman—he was Italian, I think; she was German—had just met, and settled on French as their common language. They asked each other where they were from, and where they were going. They posed each other riddles. He took out a pencil and paper and sketched her portrait. She giggled. He asked her whether she had ever considered a career as a model. She said she had considered it, but she feared that all men in the field were after the same thing. He agreed. He began to tell off-color stories. She laughed and reproached him. It was like that. I wondered whether these things were always, to captive eavesdroppers, so dreary. When I arrived at Aldo's door, he met me with a smile that seemed surprised, a little sheepish. We talked awhile. Sometimes he took, sometimes I held, my suitcase. I tried, I thought, a joke. I asked whether there was already a girl there. He said there was. He met me in an hour at the corner drugstore for a cup of coffee. We talked. We returned to the apartment. We had Scotch. That afternoon, quite late, I flew home. I called him from time to time. He had his telephone removed a few days later. Now, for a while, he's here again. He's doing a political essay. It begins, "Some things cannot be said too often, and some can." That's all he's got so far.

We had people in for drinks one night last week. The cork in the wine bottle broke. Somebody pounded it into the bottle with a chisel and a hammer. We went to a bar. I have never understood the feeling men seem to have for bars they frequent. A single-story drunk told his single story. A fine musician who was with us played Mozart, Chopin, and Beethoven on the piano. It seemed a great, impromptu occasion. Then he said, we thought, "I am now going to play some Yatz." From what he played, it turned out he meant jazz. He played it badly.

We had driven in from another weekend in the country while it was still daylight. Lots of cars had their headlights on. We weren't sure whether it was for or against peace, or just for highway safety. Milly, a secretary in a brokerage office, was married in our ground-floor shop that evening. She cried hysterically. Her mother and several people from her home town and John, whose girl she had been before he married Inez, thought it was from sentiment or shyness, or for some conventional reason. Milly explained it to Aldo later. She and her husband had really married two years before—the week they met, in fact—in a chapel in Las Vegas. They hadn't wanted to tell their parents, or anybody, until he finished college. They had torn up their Las Vegas license. She had been crying out of some legal fear of being married twice, it turned out. Their best man, a Puerto Rican doctor, said his aunt had been mugged in a cemetery in San Juan by a man on horseback. She thought it was her husband, returned from the dead. She had required sedation. We laughed. My friend across the hall, who owns the beagle, looked very sad all evening. He said, abruptly, that he was cracking up, and no one would believe him. There were sirens in the street. Inez said she knew exactly what he meant: she was cracking up also. Her escort, a pale Italian jeweler, said, "I too. I too have it. The most terrible anguishes, anguishes all in the night."

Inez said she knew the most wonderful man for the problem. "He may strike you at first as a phony," she said, "but then, when you're with him, you find yourself naturally screaming. It's such a relief. And he teaches you how you can practice at home." Milly said she was not much of a screamer —had never, in fact, screamed in her life. "High time you did, then," Inez said. Our sportswriter said he had recently met a girl whose problem was stealing all the suede garments of house guests, and another, in her thirties, who cried all the time because she had not been accepted at Smith. We heard many more sirens in the streets. We all went home.

At 4 A.M., the phone rang about fifty times. I did not answer it. Aldo suggested that we remove it. I took three Valium. The whole night was sirens, then silence. The phone rang again. It is still ringing. The paper goes to press tomorrow. It is possible that I know who killed our landlord. So many things point in one direction. But too strong a case, I find, is often lost. It incurs doubts, suspicions. Perhaps I do not know. Perhaps it doesn't matter. I think it does, though. When I wonder what it is that we are doing—in this brownstone, on this block, with this paper—the truth is probably that we are fighting for our lives.

SPEEDBOAT

"You call that ninety degrees?" he said. It was one of the many unanswerable things he used to say. I hadn't really called it ninety degrees. He had asked me to fly a ninety-degree turn. I had turned ninety-four. "Watch it. Watch it. Watch it," he said. Silence. One knows instantly, or not at all, what Watch it is a warning of. More silence. Turns. Suddenly, he grasped my wrist. I jumped. "Christ!" he shouted. "I been telling you to relax."

The students at our flight school are businessmen, veterans of Vietnam, two wives, three secretaries, a schoolboy, a Jesuit priest, and me. On clear days, the traffic over our small field is dense. Some of the veterans, who want to be professional pilots of all sorts, fly helicopters here. Planes are lined up in the sky to land, on the runway to take off. Bush pilots settle in the hills, and seaplanes on the pond. All around, helicopters keep leaping up and down. Now and then, one hears, from nowhere visible, a quavering voice. "Penrose," it says by radio, "this is Six Two Uniform. Can you help me out. I'm lost." The tower is calm. "Any familiar landmarks, Six Two Uniform?" Sorry. No. The tower asks for a description of any highways the lost pilot sees below; then, gradually, brings him in. I had not expected lost pilots to be a frequent problem in the air. I wondered, though, whether anyone, above the runway all alone, had ever feared and then refused to land. "Oh, sometimes they hesitate so long we think we're going to have to shoot them down," the instructor said. "But they run out of gas."

The instructor is irritable, nearly always. He has taught pilots in World War II and the Korean War. He considers it part of his professional manner now to bark. A natural fighter pilot can solo after his first eight hours of instruction; after flying solo for another eight, he can just plain fly. All of us would be washouts as fighter pilots, certainly. The Jesuit, who, like the instructor, studies Chinese cooking in his spare time, tried to endear himself to the instructor with the present of a wok. The instructor was briefly pleased, but his bad temper, on the whole, is incorruptible. Not since the worst, dread days of school have I heard this electric alternation of instructions to Watch it, Watch out, Pay attention, Hurry, Listen, Keep your mind on what you're doing, Hold it, Quit trying too hard, and, of course, Relax.

I fly solo these days, mostly in Three Nine Tango. I take off, turn left, turn left, turn left a third and fourth time, land, speed down the runway, take off, four lefts, land again, take off. That's what we all do; it's called touch-and-go. The reason, though, that I never practice any other thing is this: I land funny. Not roughly or dangerously, just a bit canted or askew. I am also really scared of crosswind gusts. "You don't have to *arrive*," the instructor said, bitterly, when I must have seemed to him to concentrate too gravely, on a windy day. "You're just supposed to land." Back in the early days, when we would practice stalls and spins, I nearly did give up. To stall, you deliberately climb too sharply, until you feel the engine cough. The plane shivers slightly. That's a stall. It is time to push the nose down and the throttle fully up. This process violates every natural instinct. R. D. Laing aside, it seems to be the only way to level off. Since it seems so wrong to drop a plane's nose and accelerate, when the horizon has already vanished underneath the wings and the whole machine is clearly under strain, I used to dive a bit too soon, to get it over with. "You. Didn't. Feel. No. Stall," the instructor would say, with enraged precision, as though he were about to leave and slam the door. Except that in a dive at a thousand feet, of course, he can't. "That red light was on there," I said, pointing to a small light, which was still blinking on the panel. "It says Stall." A long silence. "Nobody. Told. You. To. Look. At. Any. Light," he said.

It is no longer as clear as it was why I am in this flight school. Driving from the city to green places, it is acknowledged, takes too long. Flying is faster. Jim, who would be a less unlikely pilot than I am, says he hasn't got enough certain free hours to take it up again. There is also in my mind the memory of a poem the Speech Arts coach recited, with great feeling and the purest diction, to our high school elocution class. "Oh, I have slipped the surly bonds of earth/ And danced the skies on laughter-silvered wings/ And done a hundred things/ You have not dreamed of./ Wheeled and soared and swung/ Up, up the long, delirious burning blue," and so on. "Put out my hand and touched," the last line ended, "the face of God." Well. It wasn't Wallace Stevens. But at "touched," each time, the Speech Arts coach's voice broke. The poem had been written by a young Canadian pilot who fought in World War II. He crashed, unfortunately. Tino Bellardinelli, our All-State running back, was unmoved by this poem; he implacably chewed his toothpick. But another poem got to him. "There is something in the autumn that is native to my blood,/ Touch of manner, hint of mood;/ And my heart is like a rhyme,/ With the yellow and the purple and the crimson keeping time./ The scarlet of the maples can shake me like a cry/ Of bugles going by./ And my lonely spirit thrills/ To see the frosty asters, like a smoke upon the hills," and so on. And Agnes Betty Cotts, who had gone through the first eleven years of her schooling in some twilight of sexuality and inattention, became lofty, intellectual, and fierce with this: "So live, that when thy summons comes to join/ The innumerable caravan which moves/ To that mysterious realm, where each shall take/ His chamber in the silent halls of death,/ Thou go not, like the quarry-slave at night,/ Scourged to his dungeon, but, sustained and soothed/ By an unfaltering trust, approach thy grave/ Like one who wraps the drapery of his couch/ About him," etc. The Speech Arts coach worked with such diligence and faith on thirty juniors (who had before been known to mutter, derisively, "The Brain," when anyone so much as spoke distinctly in their midst) that all of them subsequently went to college, each with an awful favorite poem in his heart. All of us, too, stared into a profound distance and, for years, dwelled upon this problem: "For if a man should dream of heaven and, waking, find in his hand a flower as a token that he had really been there, what then? What then?"

Well, I don't know what then. Every autumn, presumably, the scarlet of the maples still thrills Congressman Tino Bellardinelli's lonely spirit like a cry/ Of bugles going by. When Agnes Betty Cotts' summons comes to join/ The innumerable caravan which moves/ To that mysterious realm, she will receive it as a nun and president of a Catholic women's college. I work here at the newspaper. Sooner or later, though, I guess I was bound to slip the surly bonds of earth/ And dance the skies on the laughter-silvered winds of Six Two Uniform or Three Nine Tango.

"Take off everything except your slip," the nurse said. "Doctor will be with you in a moment." Nobody under forty-five, in twenty years, had worn a slip, but nurses invariably gave this instruction. There they all are, however, the great dead men with their injunctions. Make it new. Only connect.

"Stop. Stop. Stop. Stop," the moderator of the talk show said. They had been taping a panel. The Indo-Chinese lesbian restaurant owner, who was holding her fish-sauces cookbook, resumed a dignified, offended silence. The crisp, cold, bracing writer was drunk, and raving to the savage pundit. The French film-archivist was talking, with delight, to the Bulgarian movie personality from California, who was about to sell, in stores across the country, the product of her secret formula for face creams. "That," said the French film-archivist, squinting through his smoke, and scattering more ashes onto his vest and trousers, "is a house of another color."

"Horse," the nine-year-old star of television commercials said.

"I know exactly what you mean," said the lady critic, who had been trying to find her way into the conversation somehow. "*Exactement* what you mean, Émile," she added, patting the Frenchman's arm. The rock musician, however, spoke at the same moment. "*Tu parles,*" he said, amiably. It was his favorite (in fact, his only) French expression. For Italians, he had "*Ecco*" and "*S'immagini;*" for Germans, "*Sowas*" and "*Unglaublich.*" He had travelled widely. In this case, he said, "*Tu parles,* Monsieur Blin."

"Stop," the moderator said again. The nine-year-old sulked.

The gentleman critic was now in his cups and muttering. Seven years ago, an obscure Southern writer by the critic's own name had been chosen for an international colloquium on modern humor, which was held in Seoul, Korea. It had not been widely covered in the press. Certainly there had been an error. Certainly the invitation had gone to the wrong —the obscure and unintended—Herbert Course. No publication, however, had called attention to the matter. In the critic's mind, the outrage had assumed immense proportions, as a parable of the monstrous in contemporary life. His divorce, his conversion to the politics and the literature of alienation had been but one result.

"Of course, you have right," said the Frenchman, in serene misunderstanding. "When I have eighteen, I go in Natalie." He seemed to be speaking of a visit to Turkish relatives in Anatolia. "I have eat something. It give me a terrible pain. In my tripes."

"Lord, yes," said the quarterback, warmly. He was already a lay preacher. He had just made a large investment in organic dog foods. The lights dimmed. The tape and the cameras had been off for several minutes. "Exhausted?" the curator of the Sixties Art Collection was saying to a cameraman who stood there. "My dear, I was drained."

I have been writing speeches for a politician. Jim, who is a lawyer from Atlanta, has been running the campaign. My normal job is reporting and reviewing at the paper. By mistake, these past few months, I also teach. Normally, left to myself, I am not inclined to work much. To the contrary. "To the contrary" is what the head of the mine workers' union said when he was asked whether he had ordered the murder of a rival and his family. It is hard to know what to the contrary of ordering a murder might, exactly, mean. Jim thinks ordering a birth, perhaps, or else a resurrection. The man was convicted anyway. I have now written "fairly and expeditiously," and "thoroughly and fairly," and "judiciously and seriously," and "care and thoroughness and honor," and so on, so many times that it may have affected my mind. I eat breakfast fairly and expeditiously. Jim cuts his own hair thoroughly and fairly. It rains judiciously and seriously, with care, and honor, and dignity, in full awareness of the public trust. Our politician, anyway, is a good and careful man—who sounds always a little pained, as though someone were standing on his foot.

Edith, from Kiev, twice divorced, and in New York, in her own words, a "terrapist," was stealing a bonbon from one of the trays on the Steinway grand. She went to the bookshelves, removed a fine old volume there, and tore the four-leaf clover pressed inside to bits. The party had not yet begun. "This Max," Franz, her own analyst, said to her next day. "How he makes you regress."

"Now here, where it says Name," said Miss Fiotti, from Fringe Benefits, "you write your name. Good. Now where it says Date. Yes. That's right. Now here, where it says Name again. Exactly. Now once more. And your signature. Wonderful. Thank you, Professor Ellis."

Miss Fiotti is the only efficient person at our city university. She is employed by the union itself. The union helps us with our forms, our insurance and pension plans, tenure, strike threats, and salaries, of course. The fact that the university is unionized at all, from janitors to deans, means that we have in many ways the worst of the civil service and of academe: a vast paper-riffling ivory tower in a cast-iron union shop. We are, in fact, a scandal citywide. Our faculty, liberal on most issues far away, sleeps well on this. Politicians tend to say the issue "does not sing." Our full professors, tenured faculty, teach H.B.A., or Hours By Appointment; that is, never. Young instructors, hoping for tenure here, are scheduled to teach days and nights. The idea is that as long as an instructor is required to be in a classroom every hour, he will not have the time to write or publish anything. Not having published, he will never earn his tenure. Under this system, instructors tend to get hepatitis and become demoralized, but, thanks to the union, they are highly paid. And so they stay.

I see Edith, Max, Franz, and Miss Fiotti every week or so. I've taught courses for two semesters here, as Ms. Associate Professor Fain. I thought I missed the academic world, the books, the hours. I took the job part-time. I noticed only gradually. One evening, in a seminar, a student spoke of the required course they had all taken with the Recording Secretary of Professor Klein. "The what?" I said. "The Recording Secretary," the brightest student said again, "of Professor Klein." Dalton Klein has been, for thirty years, a book reviewer and writer of unsuccessful musicals. I don't know what recording secretaries are. I know professors earn our professorial thirty-eight thousand a year. "Has anyone," I asked, "ever had a course with, um, with the, with Professor Klein himself?" Certainly not; even his Recording Secretary now is H.B.A. Two students within memory had, however, actually met Professor Klein; he had approved their Prior Life Experience credits—for a year they had spent raking famous people's leaves.

Prior Life Experience credits, as substitutes for courses, are one of our educational anomalies. They are normally inseparable from a less innovative program known as E.I.F. The Dean, it turns out, has a great longing to know the private phone numbers of celebrities. He hires people from newspapers, the theater, movies, television to teach. In time, he mentions the importance of having students placed with people who are already E.I.F., that is, Established in the Field. He means people who are often mentioned in the press. If one can just give him a few phone numbers, he will call them at home. I should have known. I did not understand for quite a while.

It was midnight in our paper's office building. There was a Pinkerton man in the elevator. "Something wrong?" Jim asked. "Yeah," he said. "A girl on the fifth floor has been molested."

On the television set, El Exigente was mouthing his *"Bueno,"* the natives were diving and splashing with pleasure, and Jim and I, who were never going to drink that brand of coffee, were watching the news. "His lawyer looks bored," I said. Jim reached for his drink. "You always try to look bored," he said, "when your client is committing perjury."

A lady lifted the lid of her toilet tank and found a small yachtsman, on the deck of his boat, in the bowl. They spoke of detergents. A man with fixed dentures bit into an apple. A lady in a crisis of choice phoned her friend from a market and settled for milk of magnesia. A hideous family pledged itself to margarine.

Testimony resumed. Apparently, no good lawyer permits a client who is lying to tell a long story—to perjure himself in detail. The longer the story, the more true it did seem. "Well, you had a little social conversation together, did you not?" Senator Montoya was asking. There was a short answer. "Well, did you socialize about the Watergate?" Senator Montoya insisted, in his idiosyncratic way.

"Mangia," said the lady in the lovely spaghetti-sauce commercial. *"Mangia,* Bernstein. *Mangia,* O'Malley. *Mangia,* Garcia. *Mangia,* Jones."

"Hello, Jen?" the voice on the phone said, at two one morning. "It's Mel. Sorry to call you at home." Mel is the Acting Head of our department—Drama and Cinema. The Acting Head of the Acting Department, in a way. The Permanent Head, a flustered lady of pure steel, whose academic background consists of a Midwestern degree in Oral Science and a brief marriage to an actor, is on a city grant to study Media History abroad.

"Hi, Mel," I said to the Acting Head, as warmly as I could.

"Jen, the Art Department wants to do a course in Space on Film," he said. He paused. "We knew you'd want to be informed." He paused again. "And, without trying to influence you in any way, we'd like to know what your position is." I yawned. "Mel, I feel strongly about this," I said. I had been teaching for some months. I was catching on. "I really do."

"We hoped you would," he said. "Len has just pointed out —we're having coffee here—that there are just two things on film. Time. And Space. If we let the Art people go ahead with Space, we'll have lost half . . ."

"Yes," I said. "And if the History Department takes Time away . . ."

"Exactly."

Summer. The speedboat was serious. The young tycoon was serious about it, as he was serious about his factories, his wife, his children, his parties, his work, his art collection, his resort. The little group had just had lunch, at sea, aboard the tycoon's larger boat, a schooner. The speedboat, designed for him the year before, had just arrived that day. The tycoon asked who would like to join him for a spin to test it. The young American wife from Malibu, who had been overexcited about everything since dawn, said she would adore to go. Her husband, halfway through his coffee still, declined. The young Italian couple, having a serious speedboat of their own, went to compare. In starting off, the boat seemed much like any other, only in every way—the flat, hard seats, the austere lines—more spare. And then, at speed, the boat, at its own angle to the sea, began to hit each wave with flat, hard, jarring thuds, like the heel of a hand against a tabletop. As it slammed along, the Italians sat, ever more low and loose, on their hard seats, while the American lady, in her eagerness, began to bounce with anticipation over every little wave. The boat scudded hard; she exaggerated every happy bounce. Until she broke her back.

She was sped to shore, of course, and then to Rome, by helicopter. Soon after that, she was well enough to fly back to New York. She recovered in Malibu. But violent things are always happening to the very rich, and to the poor, of course. Freak accidents befall the middle classes in their midst. Martin, our campaign contributor, who spent one term at Oxford many years ago, and who has sounded English ever since, tends to say "How *too* like life" when he is drunk. Anything—a joke, a sigh, a quarrel, an anecdote—has upon him, at such times, this effect. He says "How *too* like life." When the American lady had her accident, Martin said How too like life all afternoon.

The Dean of Cultural Affairs called a meeting of the representatives of our two departments on the question of jurisdiction in the Space on Film course, late one morning. Seven H.B.A.s attended this, because, not having thought or published anything in twenty years, and not having, like Professor Klein, careers near the mainstream of cultural life, they do not spend their lives entirely in idleness. They quarrel. The Dean, whose analyst is Franz, has the same girl who caused Edith to tear Max's four-leaf clover apart. The situation is, in every way, unorthodox. Franz was once suspended for a year from his analytic institute for having twice married his patients and divorced his wives. He spent that year as a therapist for children in our Guidance School.

Our branch of the university is accustomed anyway to jurisdictional disputes. Drama and Cinema grew out of a workshop that existed many years ago to remedy the accents of bright city girls, who could not afford college out of town. When such programs became unfashionable, the staff chose to become two faculties: Dramatistics, and Perspectives in Media. Within a year, the Media people chose to join the newer Department of Minority Groups and Social Change—which already offered History of Broadcasting 204, 301, and Seminar and whose course on Prostitution, Causes and Origins, was being televised. The Dramatistics people felt they could not attract students, or budget allocations, on their own. They added Film. Our department changed its name, and became what it now is. Our Drama people are trying to take over the English Department's course Creative Writing 101; Playwriting A. The English Literature people are beleaguered on another side. For twenty years, they have had *The Brothers Karamazov* (translated, abridged). The Department of Russian Literature, which teaches all its courses in translation now, wants Dostoevski back.

The Drama people have designs in other fields: Ibsen and

Strindberg, in particular—which seems reasonable enough, since all the texts are plays. Ibsen and Strindberg, however, belong, with Swinburne, to the Department of Germanistics and Philology. Between 1938 and 1949, all German courses were unpopular. The German Literature people simply seized Ibsen and Strindberg—and by some misunderstanding, which was noticed too late, got Swinburne as well. There were no Drama people, or any other sort of people, at that time, to compete. Chekhov, meanwhile, for reasons that, I am afraid, are clear, is taught in the Classics Department (Greek 209C). The operative principle appears to be that if any thing or person mentioned in another department could conceivably be mentioned in your own, you have at least an argument to seize the course. One night when the Women's Studies Division gets under way, we all expect there's going to be a coup.

Constituency. Dennis, a rich, unintelligent, and not particularly well-meaning man, revelled in his favorite expressions. When he was certain of something, he said it was sure as God made little green apples. When he wanted no interference from someone, he would ask him to keep his cotton-picking hands off. When he felt superior to someone, he said he ate that sort of fella for breakfast. Since a good part of Dennis' day consisted in being certain, deploring interference, and feeling superior, he had occasion to use all these idioms, which he thought gruffly witty, several times a day. His appointments secretary, in whom he confided his impressions, of business, his home life, his diet, had a recurrent dream that she shot him.

Lewis, the barber, discouraged conversation. Over the years, by keeping his face vacant and refusing to reply even to the direct questions of his customers, he managed to impose his own silence upon them. Florian, who worked the next chair, spoke incessantly and even sang sometimes. He flourished his towels. He gave advice. He danced around the little flames with which he scorched the hairstyles of his customers. As far as anyone could remember, Lewis addressed the subject of Florian only once. "Someday," he said, "I'm going to kill him."

About money. When we had come from our public schools and our private schools, and our travels abroad, and our own education to our first solid jobs in the city, one of our golden couples gave a party to raise funds. The cause was desperate and just. Five haggard members of the group whose cause it was spoke eloquently on the terrace, sang sad songs, and afterward stood among us in the living room. There were servants. There was a bartender. The first odd thing was that the cups were plastic, and the brands of Scotch, gin, bourbon, even beer, were unknown brands. We knew that charities ought not to waste money on overhead. But when the awkward moment of collection came, our most successful lawyer reached into his pocket and came up with change. One of the wives, who was just becoming known in fashion circles for her clothes, opened her purse, hesitated, and brought out a crumpled dollar bill. Checkbooks came out on every side. Checks for three dollars, two dollars, even a check for four dollars and eighty-two cents, were signed with a flourish and passed along. It became clear: nobody under forty gives anything to charity. Martin and Iris do contribute to the arts, but Martin wants to be on boards of trustees with the fathers of friends he went to Harvard with. A lot of the under-twenty-fives give every cent they have to weird sects they want to get their head together in. But nobody, as a matter of course, any longer tithes.

The Art people, then, met our people, regarding Space. The meeting began quietly enough. "I particularly resent," Mel said, leafing to the fourth page of a nine-page memorandum the Art people had sent that morning, in reply to his own eleven-page memorandum of the night before, "your use of the word 'unconscionable.' It is inappropriate in a memoranda of this sort." "Memoranda" in all departments of our university is singular, "memorandums" plural. "Phenomena" is another singular, taking the plurals "phenomenas" and "phenomenae." I have also heard "phenomenums." Usage, for those of us who went to colleges and universities of other sorts, is always odd. A change of grade, for example, after semester's end, requires of the professor a signed slip. The professor must, without the help of Miss Fiotti from Fringe Benefits, fill in the line: Reason for Change of Grade. The Dean had such a form before him as we met. "Reason for Change of Grade," it read. "Cleracal Error." It was signed "Professor Leora J. Smith." Leora is our Permanent Head.

Within three wrathful hours—in which, at one point, our people understood the Art people to have implied our people were unqualified to teach a course our people heard as Spaces, Goldwyn-Giotto: Film and Fresca—we had resolved the question of Space on Film. It will be taught jointly, by our people and their people, in a seminar next spring. It will be listed under our people in the catalogue. If anything goes wrong, the featherbedding illiterates in our department will join the reactionary pedants in theirs to blame it on Open Admissions, the program by which the university now lets all interested high school graduates in. "Open Admissions" sounds like an outdoor confessional. It is another faculty excuse for doing less and earning more. "Standards are down," the H.B.A.s and holders of degrees in Film and Oral Science will say. "We have Open Admissions, after all." I won't be here next spring.

Talent was blazing through the columns and onto the coffee tables. The physical-assault metaphor had taken over the reviews. "Guts," never much of a word outside the hunting season, was a favorite noun in literary prose. People were said to have or to lack them, to perceive beauty and make moral distinctions in no other place. "Gut-busting" and "gut-wrenching" were accolades. "Nerve-shattering," "eye-popping," "bone-crunching"—the responsive critic was a crushed, impaled, electrocuted man. "Searing" was lukewarm. Anything merely spraining or tooth-extracting would have been only a minor masterpiece. "Literally," in every single case, meant figuratively; that is, not literally. This film will literally grab you by the throat. This book will literally knock you out of your chair. "Presently" always meant not soon but now.

Sometimes the assault mode took the form of peremptory orders. See it. Read it. Go at once. Sometimes it sidled up disguised as musing, in unanswerable-question form. Shall I tell you how much I . . . Should I even attempt to describe . . . Or, should I say unequivocally . . . A favorite strategy was the paragraph-terminating: Right? Followed immediately by Wrong. This linear invitation to a mugging was considered a strategy of wit. Many sentences carried with them their own congratulations, Suffice it to say . . . or, The only word for it is . . . Whether it really sufficed to say, or whether there was, in fact, another word, the sentence, bowing and applauding to itself, ignored. There existed also an economical device, the inverted-comma sneer—the "plot," or his "work," or even "brave." A word in quotation marks carried a somehow unarguable derision, like "so-called" or "alleged." It was hard to remember yesterday's polemic, to determine whether today's rebuttal was, in fact, an answer to it. Recalling arguments in order genuinely to refute them was an unrewarding exercise. A lot of bread, anyway, was buttered on the side of no distinction. God was not dead, but the Muse was extremely unwell.

"Mutual" meant common, shared, together, both, or simply somehow two-ish, as in our mutual hope, our mutual burden, mutual decision, mutual interest, mutual advantage, perhaps mutual camping trip. "Agony" could mean anything—usually, pending indictment; physical agony, in hospitals, was called discomfort, normally. "Problem" and "personal tragedy" meant crimes. "Serene" and "out of touch with reality" meant a given speaker trying to clear himself by intimating that the boss was crazy. "He has suffered enough" meant if we investigate this matter any further, it will turn out our friends are in it, too. A sufficiency of suffering, in public life, consisted in a loss of face perhaps, or office, or, earlier, in getting caught, or having lived in dread of being caught, or in committing crimes, or having wanted to commit them. And if the real sufferer was the public man in violation of the criminal law, and a sufficiency of suffering lay in his various states of mind, then it was perhaps everyone else who got off too easily. When a new President brought our national nightmare to an end by asking us to "bind up the internal wounds," we knew that we were almost in the clear.

While people tagged up on these public codes and incantations, baby talk took over private conversation—naughty and cranky, in particular. Personal treachery and acts of violence were naughty. Citizens in the middle of small betrayals or murder trials described themselves as in a cranky mood. Murders, generally, were called brutal and senseless slayings, to distinguish them from all other murders; nouns became glued to adjectives, in series, which gave an appearance of shoring them up. The concept of the jig itself being up, however, had retreated into thrillers. Intelligent people, caught at anything, denied it. Faced with evidence of having denied it falsely, people said they had not done it and had not lied about it, and didn't remember it, but if they had done it or lied about it, they would have done it and misspoken themselves about it in an interest so much higher as to alter the nature of doing and lying altogether. It was in the interest of absolutely nobody to get to the bottom of anything whatever. People were no longer "caught" in the old sense on which most people could agree. Induction, detection, the very thrillers everyone was reading were obsolete. The jig was never up. In every city, at the same time, therapists earned their living by saying, "You're too hard on yourself."

The frail, serious four-year-old boy stood, arms outspread, at the foot of the staircase. He looked at his infant sister, who stood three steps above. "Jump, baby," he said, gravely, encouragingly. She summoned her courage, let go of the bannister, and jumped. He caught her, but since she was quite plump, she flattened him. "Good baby," he said, when his breath had returned. Then he went to his room, put on his pajamas, and lay down for his nap. Every day, when he got home from school, they repeated this process. It was his way of taking her education in hand.

At twenty-six, Kate, though not promiscuous, had slept with most of the decent men in public life. When our first campaign spokesman returned from a press conference saying, "My dears, I've never *been* so buffeted," Kate left her job at the museum and took over a lot of the campaign's hardest work. On a summer Monday, after a morning rally, Kate was walking along Forty-second Street from the subway station. She saw a tall, young, scholarly-looking man obviously about to say something to her. "Excuse me," he said at last. He said he was from the Stanford urban-contaminations study. Kate said nothing. "Sidewalks," he went on, frowning slightly. "Sidewalk contamination." He said they were working on the right shoes of pedestrians. He wondered whether he might take a slide from hers? Kate nodded. She felt a flash of unease the moment she leaned against a wall and raised her foot to take the shoe off. He was already on the sidewalk, quietly licking the sole. No passerby took any notice. In another moment, he had stood up and walked away.

Our committee, which means well but has as yet no name, no charter, and no acronym, meets every month. We drink and talk, and plan, and have dinners that begin with sherry watered down in turtle soup. At our last meeting, our distinguished painter, who is also rich, suggested that, for our next public symposium, we invite poets to speak, in prose, of their views of the contemporary world. The painter spoke at length of the unique vision poets have of things, their lack of veniality or institutional affiliation; their quality, in short, of divine ecstasy.

"Have you known many poets, Mr. Hardemeyer?" our distinguished historian, a lady, asked.

"Stacks," Mr. Hardemeyer replied.

It had been a bad day at nursery school. One of the class's six Kevins had been left in the Park. The children had been out there for an hour. The teacher noticed what she took to be a disreputable lingerer in the bushes near the pond. She went for the police. Kevin went to the statue of Alice and sat down. The teacher returned and put the children on the school bus. When they got back to the classroom, the teacher noticed she was one child short. Hysterical, she called the precinct and the mother. The officer on duty thought it best to have the mother wait at the station, while a patrolman and the teacher went back to the Park to look.

Kevin, it turned out, had climbed down from the statue of Alice and found no one. A man, probably the original lingerer in the bushes, had taken him for a walk and bought him an ice-cream cone. Kevin had not wanted an ice-cream cone especially. Having incurred enough losses in one day, he respected his obligations in the matter of adults. He returned, with his cone, to the statue, and waited to be found. The patrolman and the teacher did find Kevin. They brought him to his mother, who had behaved admirably from the first. It turned out that every single child on the school bus had known that one of their Kevins was missing. They had not mentioned it to the driver, or their teacher, or each other. They took it that Kevin had been left, forever, for some reason, which would become clear to them, with patience, in the course of time.

Here's who, of course, is out there in this city: all those Kevins (the class also includes four Wendys), the teacher, the mother, our staff at the paper, Myrnie, Lothar, the Cardinal, the committee, Lewis the barber, Mel, the unions, Bernstein, O'Malley, Garcia, Jones.

Lothar was on the board of a museum, two projects in urban renewal, a television network, a public utility, a college, a film institute, and a foundation, which, after several disheartening experiences with projects that became "controversial," confined itself to very expensive, highly critical studies of other foundations' work in dealing with the problems of the poor. Lothar knew, and was consulted by, many politicians, whom he numbered among his closest friends. When, not infrequently, two such politicians were running against each other, Lothar was asked which one he favored. "All I can tell you," he would say, "is that they are both among my closest friends." If, however, there was a considerable difference in age between two friends running for a single office, Lothar gave one to know that, consistent with his openness to ideas, he preferred the younger man.

Lothar permitted—in fact, encouraged—his wife to take an interest. Myrnie liked to travel in the South. She took part in almost all of Lothar's public-service projects. Sometimes, rarely, she had occasion to worry about Lothar's state of mind. Lothar's early upbringing had been religious, fundamentalist. He was high-church now, and had not been, in forty years, devout. An office building that he owned distressed him. It was vacant. It had been vacant for a long, long time. Myrnie noticed that Lothar was sleeping badly. It was not so much the money. Creative problem-solving had been the pride of Lothar's youth and middle age. There was, of course, the money question, too. Myrnie gave the matter thought. One evening when Lothar was at his health club, Myrnie invited the Cardinal for a drink. Myrnie and the Cardinal had met at board meetings of one sort or another. They had weathered scandals. They had been relieved, together, when the museum scandal was so rapidly replaced by the Equity Funding scandal, the Queens District Attorney

Ponzi racket scandal, the famous restaurants with sanitary violations scandal, the Boy Scouts of America local chapters padded enrollment scandal, the Biaggi testimony before the grand jury scandal, the Soap Box Derby scandal, the firemen's union strike-vote scandal—in fact, so many scandals, local, personal, and national, that it was hard to sustain attention to any single one.

Myrnie was not certain, in the case of the vacant building, what she expected the Cardinal to do, exactly. With some idea that he might levitate the building, or dissolve the spell upon it, or simply exercise his metaphysical authority in its direction, she waited for him. The Cardinal arrived, urbane, interested, but not, thank heaven, prying. He settled easily with his bourbon. With her characteristic delicacy and frankness, Myrnie outlined the problem to him. Over his second drink, he had it solved. A syndicate, of doubtful rectitude but of unquestioned financial stability, was run by an inhabitant of the diocese, who, though he had not specifically mentioned any need for an office building, most probably had such a need. One more drink, and the Cardinal departed. One more week, and the building was bought—as a headquarters for enterprises in jukebox rental, private garbage collection, and parking lots.

Lewis was an excellent barber. His customers—Lothar, Jim, Dennis, the Dean, and the Cardinal among them—held him in high regard. There was also an eight-year-old boy whose hair Lewis had been cutting once every three weeks for five years. Last week, Lewis, having completed his haircut, removed the towel from the boy's shoulders and said, "You know, you'll have to pay me."

The boy stood with his hands in his pockets. "I can't," he said. "Dad's meant to pay."

"Hasn't paid me in six months," Lewis said.

"He won't," the boy said. "Ever since he moved out, he says it's Mom's business."

"Your ma will have to pay, then," Lewis said.

"She says, under the settlement, Dad's got to pay."

"Please don't come back, then," Lewis said, "until somebody pays."

I was sitting next to the chairman of the committee, our renowned biographer. The dinner was, as it is quite often, at his club. The club is for men who have good manners and a connection of some sort with arts and letters. Twice a year, and throughout the year in selected dining rooms, the club waives its rules and lets escorted ladies in. For two courses, the chairman had pointed out to me paintings and other objects associated with high moments in the club's long history. By the cheese and salad, we had hit a lull. Mr. Hardemeyer, on my right, was muttering about "the wonderful insights of our African friends about nature." On the chairman's left, our married nun, member of the City Council, was taking down the phone number of the black psychiatrist on her left. Conversation had lapsed—definitely. The chairman and I inhaled to speak at the same moment. "You were saying?" I said. "No, please," he said. I asked whether women's groups had ever protested the exclusion of women from the club. "Ah, no," he said. "No, no. Our wives and colleagues have their own club, don't you see." "Oh," I said. The subject had been a mistake. There just aren't so many subjects. "Well, I didn't mean your wives and colleagues so much . . ." He looked alarmed, then inspired. He offered to sponsor me for membership in his wives' and colleagues' club. This involved a misunderstanding so profound that it reminded me of the time when, to surprise me on a cheerful day, Jim's brother took me, without warning, to a full performance of *Parsifal*. We gave the subject up.

The coffee table seemed to be whale vertebrae, laminated, or enclosed in Perspex. All around the wall, there were tusks. A disagreeable cat and an old gray rag were lying on the piano. A bulldog, wrapped in a blanket, wheezed on the sofa, beside the spot where a drink had been spilled. The bachelors and divorced fathers sat, with their drinks and their girls, on the floor. It was late. Now and then, someone would get up to restore circulation. Immediately, the host's fine, hard-breathing bloodhound would bound into the room. "Down," Max would say as this creature wrapped himself around another guest. "Albert," I said. "Down." There would be the sound of ice in glasses, canine panting, Max and others saying "Down," and "Shame," and "Sit."

All the men in the room had drinks in both hands. They had tried to extricate themselves from conversations by saying, "I guess I'll have another drink. May I get one for you?" The trouble with this method is that it takes people right back where they came from; it is impossible to approach with one lady's gin and tonic another lady who may be drinking Scotch. Escape procedures, however, were in full force. Some people, in a frenzy of antipathy and boredom, were drinking themselves into extreme approximations of longing to be together. Exchanging phone numbers, demanding to have lunch, proposing to share an apartment—the escalations of fellowship had the air of a terminal auction, a fierce adult version of slapjack, a bill-payer loan from a finance company, an attempt to buy with one grand convivial debt, to be paid in future, an exit from each other's company at that instant.

The inside-dopester, having been, according to the morning paper, wrong again, was ranting slightly. Edith, whose nine-year-old has polish on her nails and a silver electric chair on her charm bracelet, was on the floor in contortions, trying to endear herself to a child. "Warren *Bur*ger," the baby-food tycoon was saying to the assassination theorist. "*He's* no friend of the Establishment." A young professor from Iowa, who was in the city for a lecture series on Wordsworth and the Lake Poets, spoke of his closeness to his own students, with several of whom he had had affairs, although he did not believe, in the academic context, in shacking up. He was preoccupied with his brightest student, a girl, with whom, during office hours, he engaged in—he wished there was an Anglo-Saxon word for it—fellatio. I said I thought it was sort of a metaphor for education, wasn't it. Then I thought I had gone too far. But no. He said, "Exactly." We all watched the "Eleventh Hour News," which went on, of course, at the Twelfth Hour. Jim and I drove out to the country. It was very late. We stopped for coffee at an all-night dairy-and-diner on the way. A man got out of a truck, came in, ordered a milkshake, put his wallet on the counter, and mumbled something. Then he left, looking angry. "He asks me for a package of rubbers," the man behind the counter said. "I mean, this is a *dairy*." When our car broke down near the highway exit to the farm, a boy with a sign reading BOSTON trotted over. He thought we were slowing to give him a lift.

We may win this year. We may lose it all. It is not going as well as we thought. Posterity, anyway, does not know everything. The simplest operations of life—voting in a booth, filling out returns, remembering whether or not one has just taken a pill—are very difficult. Jim leads an exemplary life, and I can't cook. As is clear from the parking regulations, however, there are situations in which you are not entitled to stop.

ISLANDS

The driver of the island's only taxi was a tall, thin man, with almost invisible eyes and a sparse, brown, asymmetrical mustache. He drove his rickety old car in a kind of drunken weave, from one side to the other of the road. Shrill, improbable cries of "Taxi! Taxi! Taxi!" rang out from behind the rocks and hills, and from the sea. It turned out that the man was a ventriloquist. This cry of "Taxi!" was his talent, and his only joke. He required, every few seconds, to be praised for it. "Taxi!" he would scream from a passing motorbike or donkey cart. "Taxi!" from behind a cow. He insisted that his passengers laugh, turn around, look astounded, incredulous. He kept right on. If passengers resumed a conversation of their own, or gave any sign that their attention had lapsed, he would speed his car into a wilder weave, his voice into more and shriller screams. Some thought him a charming eccentric. It had never occurred to me, though, what an oddity, intellectually, ventriloquism on the radio used to be.

At the end of that summer, none of us any longer spoke any known language. Sometimes, in the presence of a Spaniard who spoke French but not English, two Americans would spend an evening talking French to him and each other. Sometimes, in the presence of an American, who naturally spoke no Portuguese, six Brazilians spent an evening talking Italian to him and each other, although the American didn't know Italian, either. Sometimes, by mistake, or having made a habit of the effort, everyone spent an evening in a language which was native to no one and inconvenient to everybody. We were under a strain. Once, a heavy man, with a thick accent or combination of accents, was brought by a young French actress to dinner. He was introduced as Boris. He said he was a doctor. When someone asked what sort of doctor, he said "mnnh, mnnh, an healer," with an "h" as though someone had thrown him a medicine ball. His work, he said, made use of what he must call the most mnnh, mnnh healing words in any language. "The Lord is my shepherd," he began. "I have not want. He teach me to lie down in the green. Vast, He leads me still to the water. He restore there my soul. Mnnh, hah, yea though . . ." he rumbled profoundly through to the end. Nobody knew quite what to say to him. Later, when I found myself sitting beside him on a couch, I asked him what his nationality was. His answer was long and deep. I did not understand a word. I asked him what his first language had been. Another intense monologue. I didn't get it either. I tried another route. What language now, I asked, came to him most easily. "Mnnh, mnnh, ah," he said, sipping his vodka and managing to breathe, at the same time, insinuatingly, "I speak the language of love."

The island had no trees. Rocky and bleak, with patches of living scrub and patches of burned and blackened scrub, it floated in the ocean like a worn-out Brillo pad. There were bandits in the interior, and farms with goats that fed on the few green things in the dry dirt among the rocks. The islanders did not care for the coast. They feared the sea. They did not fish. They could not swim. They thought of the sea as a source of malaria. Forty years ago, American scientists on a grant had eliminated malaria from the place. Still, the island fathers, distrustful for generations of the shore, always left to their sons the goat-farming interior lands, and to their daughters the unfarmable coast. The result was that, when the jet outriders came, with their boats, and their architects, and their search for an unspoiled sea, the island women began to sell their beaches and became extremely rich. They still dressed in black, and their teeth were bad. But they travelled, by plane, to the mainland from the new airport. They shopped in Ostia, Torino, and Rome. Within ten years, their sons and husbands had spent all the rest of the money, on cars, appliances, and schemes to become richer still. They were poor again.

The jet outriders had, by this time, built their houses. The rest of the coastline was owned by consortiums. Hotels were going up. The island sons and daughters now took jobs in the tourist hotels. Bandits remained active in the interior. On the coast, in the houses of the outriders, a Communist party formed. The party swept through the staff of the hotels too, of course; but hotel employees ran a risk of being fired, which was not shared by servants in the private houses. The owners spent so much of the year away. The uniformed couples in those lovely houses, then, became the party leadership. Hotel waiters, waitresses, maids, bell captains and porters, party members all, remained wary of management, of mandarins in the front office, and above all, of the cooks. The cooks were mad, short-tempered, morose, individualistic, and elitist to the core. But, particularly in the off-season, the hotel cadres found it possible to come to the meetings, in the kitchens and living rooms of the absent rich, of their party cells.

We did not see Boris again after the night we met him. We did not see the actress again, either. Mixed as we all were on our coast, and in our house, we began to take a shine to expressions, adopting words and phrases from each other all the time. "*Écoute,*" Marge Brown would say to her four-year-old and to her husband. "*Écoute,* Bunny. Joe, please. *Écoute.*" Everyone swore continuously. English was the language for that. Elio Kahn's French was perfect, except for his accent, which was terrible. He cultivated this terribleness. It suited his humor. His precise French, pronounced in flat-out American Southern, also gave what he said a kind of slow burning quality, as though his words had their own built-in double take. One evening, when we were on a neighbor's terrace, one of the coast's most beautiful young wives walked dreamily by. Marge remarked that she looked older. Joe said she looked dissolute. Even Greg, who seldom talks at all, said it seemed she'd put a lot of mileage on. And Elio, Elio just leaned back and said, "Well, yes. She does look *un peu défraîchie.*" Greg, who had spent the winter in a Patmos monastery, had a single Greek word: *Oreia.* It seemed to be an exclamation of approval or joy. He used it incessantly, in a tone so flat, bleak and despairing that we all began to like it. *Oreia,* we would say, when the waiter, after four hours, brought our dinner. *Oreia,* when, after nine straight days, the rain stopped. *Oreia,* when the radio, which was dead most nights, woke up and spoke the news.

We were not exactly hated on the island—or if we were, it was likely that everyone else was hated more. We were not exactly homeowners, not tourists, not celebrities, expatriates, or hippies, not exactly anything. We were not always there at the same time. None of us ever stayed long. We were not there out of boredom. We had all been coming there, from our separate directions, for so many years.

The first year I ever came to the island, there was no phone and no hot water. Since there was no electricity, there were no lights. I was alone; I had rented a house. During the month in which I had the house, the road was being moved. Electricity and telephones, it was said, could not be installed even in town until the road was done. My house, for some reason, was built straight down a hill, in a kind of shaft. One entered through the kitchen, the highest point, and then almost immediately fell down three flights of stairs. The walls on the sides of the stairs were covered with framed, glass-enclosed butterflies. Three mornings a week, a woman came to clean. What she spoke was not exactly Italian, not exactly Spanish, not exactly anything. It was local, a result of all the many invasions and immigrations the island had undergone since before the Crusades. She was squat and, normally, sullen. She wore a wide black skirt, a black blouse, sandals and woolen socks. The only sign of animation she ever gave occurred when she spoke of the men who were working on the road. They were from the interior. Darkly, she mentioned their violent, wrathful dispositions, their criminal natures, the atrocities it was their custom to commit. It was a matter of absolute necessity to them, she would assure me, a matter of absolute, hideous, interior, criminal necessity for these men to commit atrocities. For example, and here her own face would assume an almost maniacal slyness, for example, I might have heard chanting on certain mornings, at sunrise? I might have heard it? On such days, the men in the work crews were strangling a cat. No, she could not believe it either; the children had seen it. Here she called Antonio, her nine-year-old. Yes, he had seen it. From their interior, criminal necessity, these men required, at dawn sometimes, to strangle cats. And so, this was her normal peroration, I should take care. That was all, that was what she would say to me: I should take care.

Private Aufrichtig was the son of immigrants from Rumania. He had graduated from a yeshiva and from college in Queens. He was planning to become a C.P.A. Private Lehmann was the son of a famous novelist and an opera singer. He had gone to Exeter and Harvard. He wrote plays. Both men, one through his brother-in-law's contacts with a local politician, the other through his father's friendship with a retired army general, had managed to avoid the draft, with just four months' active service in the National Guard. Their names had been jumped to the top of the lists at their local armories. There they were. At five o'clock on a morning in February, their third morning as Guardsmen, Privates Aufrichtig and Lehmann had been ordered to clean the barracks floors and stairs. They had already been working forty minutes, on two flights. The mops and brushes, even the soap and water, seemed, like the rest of the Guard equipment, worn and obsolete. Both men were haggard and tired. Both men were cold. On a step near the top landing, Private Aufrichtig turned to his colleague, sighed deeply, and spoke his first words of the morning. "Ach, Lehmann," he said. Private Lehmann replied, without hesitation, "Ach, Aufrichtig."

Aufrichtig, Lehmann, all the recruits at the base had been through three weeks of their training; they had marched, and stood guard, and cleaned up, and attacked, and marched more. They were tired and fit. They had also sat through evenings of lectures. On their third Thursday, they were lectured on venereal disease. There was a long talk by a sergeant. There were slides and a movie. The movie was harrowing in its physical detail. When the movie was over, the sergeant returned to the platform. "All right, men," he said. "Now, Dessalines has had this thing, haven't you, Dessalines? Dessalines, stand up." A stocky recruit, looking foolish, stood up. "You've had this thing, haven't you, Dessalines?" said the sergeant. "Yes, sir," the recruit replied. "Sit down," said the sergeant. Dessalines sat down. "All right, men," the sergeant said. "Be alert."

Be alert, near the army base; on the island, take care. When Lehmann, Dessalines and I were still at the same public school, Miss McKenny used to conclude each year's American History Week, in every senior class, with a discourse. It ranged in subject from the treachery of Roosevelt in getting us into that war to save his Russian friends to the sinister effects those Russians, and their colleagues, and their co-religionists, must already have upon our thoughts. And so, class, was her yearly final sentence to us, Don't say you have not been warned. We never said it. Nobody I ever met who grew up in the fifties, Lord knows, would have said it, could properly claim on any subject whatsoever not to have been warned.

The Europeans, having tried various spas in their lifetimes —Ischia for its mudbaths and nightlife, Baden-Baden for its hotel and waters—came to the clinic of Doctor Schmidt-Nessel out of a new conviction that the best evidence for the soundness of a cure must lie, after all, in the longevity of the man by whom it is run. Doctor Muehsam, who had died the previous summer, not of his extreme old age, but of a mysterious fall down six flights of stairs in his clinic (mysterious because, since the flights were separated by landings, Doctor Muehsam must have continued his fall around corners; also, because he had left the clinic, not to his wife, who had helped him to run it, but to his directress of gymnastics, a nurse), had disappointed them, by dying. However, he had always looked a frail and burning man. Doctor Schmidt-Nessel, who was bearded, vigorous, and by his own account well over ninety, gave no sign of ever passing on.

Schmidt-Nessel, whose waiting list was long, believed most strongly in the therapeutic, life-sustaining properties of dew—to be, in serious cases, drunk at breakfast, and in all other cases, skipped around in, on the lawn. He believed also in the efficacy of chants. As a result, just before dawn each weekday morning, all patients of whatever age lined up, barefoot, in the Alpine grass, in a sort of conga-line formation, and skipped together, chanting *Nu Na Neu Won* (short for *Nun Nahen Neue Wonnen,* Now Near New Raptures), and *Wir Stammen Von Dem Liebesquell* (We Spring From the Love Source) to the morning sun. A young woman, whose husband had sent her to the clinic because of her asthma, began to laugh at the second chant, on her second morning. She was expelled. Laughter, however, was one of Schmidt-Nessel's remedies; he required only that it be in prescribed and chanted form. A schoolteacher, who had come because of her nerves, arrived a few minutes late for the Laugh Chant on her first morning. Not having been apprised of there being such a thing as a Laugh Chant, and hearing a unison of derisive laughter when she came through the doorway, she took it that she was being laughed at, and went to pieces entirely.

Every Tuesday night, however, Schmidt-Nessel had a special cure for the Nervous Cases. One of his beliefs was that people in the modern world do not breathe properly; that one of the ways to get them to breathe properly is to make them gasp; and that one way to make them gasp is to hit them. On Tuesday nights, Schmidt-Nessel dealt with the Nervous Cases in the cellar, where he sprayed them, one by one, with a high-powered hose. The schoolteacher, who had not been told about this ritual, either, found herself, first, lined up naked in a concrete room full of naked strangers, then alone with the doctor in a small cubicle, where water slammed her against one wall and another until she began to cry hysterically. Two patients from Albuquerque, worried, sent someone downstairs to ask what the trouble was, and whether Schmidt-Nessel was quite certain that this treatment was right. Doctor Schmidt-Nessel, sitting, immense, in his black bikini, on a cinder block in the steam-filled cubicle, did not deign immediately to answer. Later, when he was dressed, he pointed out to the couple from Albuquerque that if he were a surgeon they would not presume to put to him questions of this sort. They thought it over, and set out for home the following evening. The schoolteacher pulled herself together, presumably breathed deeply, and left by the same train. In the end, in Albuquerque, the schoolteacher married Harry's and May's oldest son. That's Aldo's friend and partner back in Hartford. Often, when we are not on this island, they are here.

There is a difference, of course, between real sentiment and the trash of shared experience. "I remember you. In first grade, you told Miss Hennebery that Dan Frayne, the class albino, and I had been whispering during Silent Meditation. The next winter, you showed me a wino exhibitionist in our local railroad station. You said he had VD, which was the day we won the war in Europe, and that my Uncle Jean, who had fought in France, would be just like him. I went away to school for some years. In 1954, you ran over my dog. We did not meet again until after college, when we were both in love for a time with the same man at the law office where I worked. Since then, you have told any number of false and vicious stories at my expense. Now we meet again," is not to say, "Know each other? Gosh, we've been close for thirty years."

So, when you find yourself sitting in a bomb shelter beside someone who refuses to share either of two blankets with a small child who is shivering; or you find yourself standing in a living room beside someone who, seeing a sad, powerful, distinguished man, recently widowed, in animated conversation with a shy, young, not quite homely woman whose husband has left her, when you find yourself standing beside someone who then swoops toward the gentleman, embraces him as though he were a lover swum out to save her from a cruel drowning, and saying "Darling, I've been so longing to talk to you," protracts her embrace until she has removed him from the not quite homely woman, as effectively as a sheepdog might single out a sheep or a tackle might crowd a runner out of bounds at the sidelines—when, time and again, such a person happens to be, in fact, the same one, it is best not to think, nostalgically, "Hell, we've been through a lot together," unless you are prepared to add, "You have caused, over the years, varieties of unhappiness for which I have not, perhaps, been sufficiently grateful."

When we were still in graduate school in England, Aldo used to read his Aristotle, for a time, before he went to sleep. When he turned the bedside lamp off, he used to drop this Aristotle on the floor. A few months later, we became friends with the downstairs tenants, also students. They spoke of the eccentricities of the previous tenant of our place. He gave enormous drunken parties. He threw watermelon rinds into the garden. Once, he had himself climbed naked into the garden, and sung a song there, until the neighbors complained; two of his guests had climbed down and lifted him back through the window. It had seemed to them that this tenant never slept. "Could you just tell us, though," Kate said, one evening after dinner, "what is that final nightly thud?"

The eight-year-old Greek boy had been sitting on the toilet since dawn. He left the door open, so that he could watch the events in the awakening house. Each morning at five, there was a tremendous braying, squawking, mewing, barking in the street. The mules were climbing the hill and annoying the cats and the chickens. The mongrel dogs all over the hillside became hysterical. The roosters, which had crowed intermittently all through the night, gained confidence that day had, in fact, arrived, and began to crow incessantly. The noise of the mosquitoes had, at least, subsided, by the time the boy assumed his watch from the toilet seat. At eight-thirty, his grandmother called him to the kitchen. What she did in the kitchen was never clear. In theory, she was the maid. She could not cook. The point of cleaning seemed in some way to escape her. The principle that you take a clean thing to wipe a dirty thing, that the formerly clean thing becomes thereby a thing to be washed in its turn—this principle was, every morning, seriously confused. In any case, when his grandmother called him, the boy went to the kitchen. I went to the lavatory and flushed. I flushed again. All over the house, people sat up, startled, in their beds. Between sixteen and twenty-two Americans had been staying there all month. Five were sleeping in the dining room, four on each of the two terraces, no less than three in any bedroom, and a few others scattered elsewhere about the house. There were only two bathrooms; water was expensive. It had been agreed that no one would ever overfastidiously flush. Few people in the house woke up much before noon. Most stayed up on the terraces until four every morning, drinking and looking at the sky. I brushed my teeth. I went to the kitchen, put on water for coffee, and got a cup of yoghurt from the refrigerator. The grandmother and the boy stood there and smiled. I wiped off the breakfast table with a sponge. I sat reading a thriller in the sun.

By nine o'clock, Lyda awoke. Lyda likes houses; she is good with them. She went directly to the kitchen, where, every morning, in a monologue, accompanied by many gestures, she gave the maid what were meant to be the household's instructions for the day. The grandmother did not understand a word, or care to. Her daughter, whom Lyda considered less intelligent, was by this time standing in the kitchen, too. It was hard to understand on what basis Lyda made any evaluation of mother and daughter in terms of intelligence; neither had ever given a sign of comprehending even the other. But the daughter responded to any request or instruction with an expression that suggested that, while she did not understand a single word, she had never heard such degrading, stupid, insane words in her life. She conveyed this impression by causing her head to loll forward, her mouth, with the corners down, to hang open, while she exhaled in indignation and contempt. Then, she would utter her single, all-purpose syllable, "Buh." After the daughter had done several tones of "buh," ranging from incredulity to outrage, the mother would begin winking, with little conspiratorial smiles, while she pronounced a range of monosyllables of her own. This may have been meant to imply that the mother was, in fact, obliging. Mother, daughter, and eight-year-old were, however, consistent in never obliging Lyda, or anyone, in anything. The household lived that month on drink, the local yoghurt, sometimes eggs, and an impromptu parody of wartime rations: Spam omelet, breaded cucumbers, sprat casserole.

In almost every thriller, a point is reached when someone, usually calling from a phone booth, telephones with a vital piece of information, which he cannot divulge by phone. By the time the hero arrives at the place where they had arranged to meet, the caller is dead, or too near death to tell. There is never an explanation for the reluctance of the caller to impart his message in the first place. Certainly, the convention existed well before the age of the tape recorder and the wiretap. Not on the phone, in a spy or mystery story, has always been, in and of itself, sufficient to hold up the resolution of a case for a long, long time. This is particularly remarkable in the sense that when, at last, the hero is able to imagine, project, or piece together the message of the original caller, that message invariably consists of a very few words. Joe did it. Or, Not I. Or, The League. The trouble with islands is that such cases, of necessity, go unsolved there. When there is no phone.

The dyes from the paper factory were seeping downhill to the gelatin factory, creating blue, brown and even dappled jello, and serious litigation over water rights. That was two miles inland. On the hill directly above the port, the young shipowner, who loved the view over his flowers to the ocean, set sprinklers in the garden every morning. His neighbor downhill and to the right made various claims about this water: that it seeped down in such a way as to undermine the foundations of his house; that it cascaded down in such torrents that his dog had nearly drowned; that his children were threatened; that dog and children had already suffered colds and incurred psychological harm. These claims were set forth each day in long, elegantly composed and increasingly vituperative letters. Every evening, the young shipowner wrote his own elegant, but after a time witty and brief replies. Although the houses were not many yards apart, the correspondence was carried on by the regular post. When the postal employees joined in the island's wave of general strikes, the letters were interrupted, as was everything.

Back here, the enmity began when the tenant on the third floor, an early riser, stole the *Times* of the tenant on the fifth. On weekdays, the third-floor tenant would acquire his paper honestly, along with his cigarettes, on the way to the school where he was a history teacher and guidance adviser to the senior class. He was a bachelor. On Saturday mornings, he would escort whoever had spent the night with him to her own place; or, if he had spent the night at her place, he would return alone. In either case, he would buy a paper on the way. On Sunday, however, and within a few months of the first occasion every single Sunday, he would steal his upstairs neighbor's *Times*. The first theft had been, in a way, accidental. He had assumed, from the silence on the staircase all weekend, that the fifth-floor couple were away. He was wrong. The fifth-floor husband, having come down to the sidewalk, and found his newspaper missing, ranted all the way up the stairs to the fourth floor, where he paused for breath. I live on the fourth floor. The third-floor tenant, as he subsequently explained to me, thought this humorless of our neighbor. Some weeks, he stole the whole paper; some weeks, just the News of the Week in Review. I don't think there is a reader of the Sunday *Times* in the world who does not, every Sunday, experience some anxiety that his News of the Week in Review section will be missing. The fifth-floor tenant was beside himself. It is possible that there will be murder, in the end.

She did not know the way. They had arrived for dinner in their separate cars, never having before, as it happened, met. They had drinks and dinner. When it was time to leave, the hostess, remarking that they both lived in the same neighboring town, and knowing Marge's sense of direction to be poor, suggested that Joe lead the way back. So they drove through the night, he in his old Packard, she in her battered Ford. Along the curves of the back road, on the highway, on the dark back roads again, she maintained the distance between them perfectly. When a car passed her, and seemed about to stay behind him, she passed the car easily in her turn. Watching at intervals, for miles, through the rearview mirror, he saw her driving smoothly, keeping that steady distance; he had not needed to slow down. It turned him on.

Years ago, when we were not even the same people, years and a lot of separations ago, Aldo and I went to the particular bar in Venice where he and his friends had gone all one summer, when they were still boys, at boarding school. The bar was not crowded. Italian workingmen came in, had one quick drink, and left. There were only four bar stools. Aldo and I sat down. We ordered drinks. Aldo was certain the bartender recognized him, that he was holding back any sign of recognition until the regular customers were gone. Over our third drink, Aldo began to speak his Italian, of which he was proud then. After a time, the bartender, who turned out also to be the owner, did remember, or claimed to remember, the young Americans who had come to his bar so often, seven years ago. He called to a back room, to his two brothers, who came out and sat on the stools beside us. Aldo ordered Scotch all around. He was congratulated many times on his fluency in Italian. The brothers pronounced it incredible for one who had spent so short a time in Italy. He was, for a moment, hurt by the qualification. Then he took it to be a joke, and happily smiled. One more round of Scotch. Then, the bartender, with solemnity and in friendship, brought out the house brandy and treated us to a drink. The house brandy was greenish brown, with the texture of the filling in a many-year-old bonbon. It seemed, after all those drinks, not bad. It was also the particular house drink that Aldo remembered with such fondness. Seeing how happy the first glass seemed to make him, the brothers insisted that we drink several rounds of it.

Our *pensione* was extremely squalid. I have no memory of crossing Venice to return to it, although we did get there. The *pensione* was not on any canal. It is probable that we walked. We were the only transients. There were six permanent tenants, women, staying in the place. They were not young. They wore black. They sat, most of the time, in the dark parlor, which had stained, stuffed chairs on a floor of dirty linoleum. They discussed us. Sometimes they fell silent when we came in. Sometimes not. Often we heard them through the wall of our bedroom. I was certain, it only stood to reason, that they also heard us. Aldo said that was paranoid. If they heard us, that was their problem. He had to like the place. It was the one they had all stayed in that boarding-school summer. Or he thought it was. And if it wasn't, it was certainly like it. Or near it, anyway. It wasn't the sort of neighborhood you could forget. From the moment we first arrived, in any case, and gave the concierge, or proprietress, or whatever she was, our separate passports, and she hesitated, and then thought what she could charge and decided to admit us, it was clear that the six old Venetian women had a lot to talk about.

When we got back to the *pensione* from the bar with the house brandy, we went through the parlor to our room. We went to bed. Late that night, I woke up. Sick. Sicker than I had ever been in my life before, or have been since. There was a small sink in our room. Within a short time, I had exhausted the possibilities of this sink. The *pensione* had only one lavatory. Under somewhat better control, I managed to put on Aldo's raincoat and go there, to be sick. Then, I went back to our room, tidied up, brushed my teeth at our sink, went to bed and passed out. When I woke up, just at dawn,

I felt almost well. It seemed only right to check on the condition of that lavatory, though, before the other guests got up. Aldo was still asleep, I thought, but looked healthy. I found my own trench coat this time, and set out down the hall. Four of the women were in the doorways of their rooms; the other two sat in chairs they had put outside the lavatory door. They stared. They smiled. They clucked. It seemed somehow horrible. The lavatory was clean. I walked back to our room. The woman across the hallway nodded, cooed, made a cradling motion with her arms, and said, very slowly and distinctly in Italian, Perhaps he will marry you now. I smiled at her. I went into our room and shut the door.

Maybe it was a hangover. It was certainly the most wretched moment of my life. I got back into bed. Aldo moved, woke up, groaned. "I feel awful," he said. I said I did too. The house brandy, I thought. He shook his head. He did look worrier, sadder even, than I had ever seen him look. He said, "I don't know whether I can tell you." It was unlike him. For a minute, I thought he was leaving, then realized he wasn't. "It's only me," I said. He said, "Well, you especially. I don't know what you'll think." He asked me to look away. I shut my eyes. He coughed. He said, "I made love to you. While you were out cold." Pause. I said, "No. I remember. I would have thought I was awake." He said, "I don't mean then. Later." I didn't say anything. He said, "Twice." I waited. Silence. I said, "Well, I guess I missed it then." He said I honestly didn't have to be as nice as that about it. He clearly meant that. Miserable as I was for my own reasons, I could tell he did mean that, whatever it was. I said, "Well, I guess I don't understand." He said, "You don't?" I said, "No." He said, "Really?" I didn't say anything. He coughed. He said, "Necrophilia." So I was in despair because six fat women of Venice I would never see again thought I was pregnant by a man who did not want to marry me, and he was in despair because he thought he was a necrophiliac. Both despairs were genuine. It may be that we were retarded.

We were younger. We were other people, anyway, in another world.

Some images yellow and dry out like parchment. Some casts of mind become obsolete. "And fold their tents like the Arabs, and silently steal away," for instance, is a thoroughly dated idea. In its obituary of King Faisal, the *Times* mentioned, as an example of his modernism, the fact that in the 1930s he abolished slavery. As an example of his gift for poetry, there was the line, "See you. There be Arab." Something lost in translation there, perhaps. Everywhere.

Three holidays. On New Year's Eve in Zurich, it is customary to bring in a live and healthy piglet. Precisely at midnight, everyone kisses it on the snout. While this occasions what seems to be terror in the piglet, it is meant to bring people a year of luck. One year, my parents and I were, on a New Year's Eve, in Zurich. We were having dinner in a hotel restaurant. The other guests, except for the Germans, had all been relatively restrained through dinner, although most people seemed to be drinking steadily. Shortly after eleven, there was, at all the tables, that awful and rising tension. It grew. People drank more. At one minute to twelve, a dignified old headwaiter dashed in through the doors of the kitchen. The piglet was struggling under his arm. At midnight, he began to hold it out to one guest after another. Nobody seemed to skip it. Some people shyly or desultorily pecked at it. Some people seemed actually reverent about it, as though they were praying or making a wish. Some of the young Swiss and Germans who were drunkest tried to turn the thing into an amorous joke. Distinguished-looking men tried to look as though they didn't care one way or another about it. But everyone was kissing the snout of that struggling pig. My mother was worrying about germs, but very apparently worried. When the piglet got to her, she hesitated a moment, then kissed the tip of her finger and touched the piglet's nose. That seemed to lighten other people's quandaries. I just patted the piglet. A couple at the only table that came after ours just gave it a hug.

In a public school in a run-down section of Brooklyn, Mrs. Cavell, under a grant for special projects, was conducting her kindergarten civics class. "What are you?" she would say to her little people, right after the bell each weekday morning. "I'm free," they had learned to say, as one. On a particularly cold, bleak morning of midwinter, Mrs. Cavell tried a variation. "Today, we are going to say it in our individual voices," she said. "When I call on you, I want you to stand and say it proudly. All right. Jefferson Adams, what are you?" Jefferson Adams got it. "I'm free," he replied. "Right. What are you, Franklin Atell?" "I'm free," Franklin Atell said. Mary Lou Jones had to be asked to speak up, but then she said it firmly, "I'm free." Up and down the rows of carved and gum-stuck desks in the pre-school classroom, the words rang out, but Mrs. Cavell, a good soul, who had taught for thirty years in Brooklyn, saw a look of somehow disquieting resolution on Billy Martin's face. "What are you, Billy Martin?" Mrs. Cavell asked. "I am four," he said.

The Piano. The rich grandmother was always giving her grandchildren presents which had to be put away until the children were old enough to care for them properly. On one birthday, the five-year-old was given his great-grandfather's pocket watch; his twin sister was given an extremely fragile eighteenth-century doll. As a reward for giving up chewing gum, the seven-year-old—who had reached such an intensely tomboy phase that, although she was constantly on playing fields or in the trees, she refused to change out of a single set of clothes, or to permit them to be washed—was given a strand of pearls. For his graduation from grammar school, the twelve-year-old received shares in a utility. On other occasions, this grandmother bought expensive clothes or gold wristwatches, invariably in her own size, which she gave to the children with the suggestion that they grow into them.

The other grandmother, who was poor, took the children to the five-and-ten and gave them things that could be put to immediate use. She was, perhaps unfairly, far the more popular grandparent of their early years. Twenty years passed.

At Christmas, in this country, as before in Germany, the family did not have a tree. Not being at all devout, however, and having grown over the years to a considerable number, including one great-grandmother and seven small children, the family had to make some accommodation to the season. This accommodation became increasingly festive and odd. Christmas was called Christmas, but it was celebrated on any day in December when the entire family could make it, could return conveniently from their separate places to the country house where the grandparents lived. This day seldom, any longer, fell on December 25th. Decorations were eclectic. Presents were placed, in fact, on and under the piano—an old Steinway grand that no one any longer played. Out of a vague conviction that the youngest children ought to be reminded that they were not really quite Christians, their grandmother yearly lighted candles on the eight-branched silver holders, which she had inherited from her own grandparents, and which were polished for whatever day was the designated Christmas of the year. The maid, however, a strong-minded Catholic, felt the occasion was too bleak with just those frail and flickering candles. Yearly, she placed more ribbons, tinsel, twigs, pine cones, and finally colored light bulbs on the piano and around its base. The year she put a painted wooden angel on top of the largest present on the piano, it was thought that she had gone too far. The angel was removed.

The presents were an annual disappointment. The great-grandmother, who approached the occasion with the highest expectations, liked to unwrap, not just her own presents, but everyone's. Among the youngest children, this sometimes brought tears. The grandfather, who pretended not to care about the holiday, every year, until the precise moment when the door to the study, where the piano stood, was opened and the presents were revealed, became, every year, at that moment, hopeful, eager, even zealous, and then dejected, utterly. No one had ever found a present that actually pleased him. "Very nice," he would say, in a tight voice, as he unwrapped one thing after another. "Very nice. Now I'll just put that away." The year his sons gave him an electric razor, he said, "Very nice. Of course, I'll never use it. I'm too old to change the way I shave." When they asked him at least to try it, he said, "No, I'm sorry. It's very nice. Now I'll just put that away." Everyone in the family, through a run of years, had taken this reaction as a challenge, to find him something, anything. But from the years of the clay ashtrays, through the year in the war when his nine-year-old son somehow bought him an object, at the fair, called a butter stretcher, to the years of things in gold, scrapbooks, and family poems, he was, for his own reasons but like almost everyone else, as saddened by Christmas as though the world had died.

What everyone dreaded was the birthday song. Anthems are sung in crowded halls. You can stand and mouthe. Carolers and singers from the *Fireside Book* are volunteers. You can stand and smile at them, or go away. But when the birthday song is imminent, the group is small. There is the possibility that everyone will mouthe. Someone begins firmly, quavers. Others chime in with a note or two, then look encouragingly, reprovingly, at the mouthing rest. The mouthers release a note or two. The reprovers lapse. The thing comes to a ragged, desperate end. If the birthday person's name is Andrew or Doris, the syllables at least come out. Otherwise, you can get Dear Ma-ahrk, or Dear Barbarasoo-ooh, or a complete parting of the ways—some singing Herbert, some Her-erb, some Herbie, and, if the generations and formalities are mixed enough, Herbert Francis, Uncle Herbles, and Mr. Di Santo Stefano. The song is just so awful, anyway. I cannot imagine, though, from what the double shyness about singing, about being seen *not* to sing derives. There seems to be no early trauma that would account for it. Someone may accuse a small child of being unable to carry a tune, although I've never heard of this; but surely no one then insists that the poor child be seen to mouthe. Then, then, just when the song has faltered to its abysmal close, the birthday person inhales somewhere near the candles of that hideous pastel cake, inhales, perhaps singes his mustache or gets frosting on his tie, gets wax onto the cake or, if it is a she, into her hair, sprays everything with the exhaling breath. Applause. But it may well be that having no respect for occasions means having no respect for the moment, after all.

The onset of the state of mind consisted in a loyalty to objects. She apologized to one egg for having boiled it, to another for not having selected it to boil. Since it was impossible to know with much precision whether an egg prefers to be boiled or not to, she was always in a state of indecision, followed, as soon as she had taken any action, by extreme remorse. Since this is not far from the predicament of most people of any sensitivity or conscience, she passed for normal. It was not immediately apparent that her oscillation between regret and indecision was brought on as much by this matter of the claims and preferences of objects as by more ordinary moral quandaries. When these oscillations began to shatter her sleep and her poise entirely, it became clear something must be done. What we did was to leave her alone. Vlad told us one evening of two patients in a state asylum. One was catatonic, the other melancholic. The catatonic, like catatonics, just sat there. For years. But, also like catatonics, when once, after all those years, he bestirred himself, he did so with enormous energy and force. He tore his iron bedstead apart. He rushed into the next room and hit the melancholic, with tremendous force, upon the head. The catatonic relapsed. But the melancholic, from shock and surprise presumably, recovered. When Jane was mildly struck by a Vespa, her aphasia and craziness went. She was fine.

One more island, this one in the Caribbean. Our nationalities were mixed, as usual. Hendon was English, handsome in a way that was somehow flat and imbecilic. His sandy forelock was always in place. His eyes were green. His hands were long, with very broad, flat fingers. He wore bathing shorts, with vertical stripes in rainbow colors. Quite late every morning he appeared on the beach with his girl, a tall, dark, thin person in black. It was said that she was one of the most highly paid models in England. Her presence with Hendon on the island had to be kept secret from anyone back home. Any home. It turned out that she had, in fact, been a model in London tabloids. It never did become clear why her secret must be kept. But visitors to the island were always rumored to be one of the best, or most highly paid of something, and preferably to have some mystery as well. Of Hendon it was said, and he cheerfully confirmed it, that he had spent nine years in English prisons, for the crime of having inflicted "grievous bodily harm." A nine-year sentence meant that he had done his work extremely thoroughly. He had been a gang enforcer. He had beaten several men almost to death. The explanation would have been enough to include Hendon among the other best and most and mysterious members of the beach group, but he had another quality. Whenever he was asked to, and often when he wasn't, he would pull down the front of his bathing suit and flash. He did this quickly and somehow discreetly. He did not dwell on it. He would pull up his trunks again at once, politely laugh. People began to call him the flasher. Jokes were made about the sexual honor of the white visitors among the black islanders. Other jokes like that.

On the day the Queen was to arrive on the island, all the islanders gathered at the airport—which consisted of a shack and one runway of not altogether smooth tarmac. When everyone had arrived, by jeep or on foot, the governor of the island arranged them in an L-shaped line. The base of the L was parallel to the shack, and stood facing in the direction from which the plane would land; the spine of the L stood along the runway itself. Hendon and his girl stood in the base line, with the few whites who knew the Queen already and the few blacks who were island officials. Some people wore bathing suits. Some people wore sports clothes. Some people, mostly the island blacks, wore dresses, or suits and ties. Hendon was in his striped, many-colored bathing suit. There was the sound of an engine rumble in the sky. The plane appeared from the wrong direction, then circled and landed as it should. Everyone waved as it taxied down the runway. Hands could be seen to wave at the small plane's window. The door opened. Pilot and passengers got out. Hendon flashed for the Queen.

There was, of course, no way of knowing whether the Queen had noticed. With her lady-in-waiting, and a tall man who appeared to be limping, she paused to shake hands with everybody. The governor introduced Hendon as the flasher. The Queen gave no sign. She shook his hand. When she had said hello to everyone, and gone with her group, by jeep to her house on the tip of the island, Aldo and I somehow got into the jeep with Hendon and his girl. The girl drove. Hendon was in a fugue state. He began an intense monologue, the gist of which was that the Queen had class. "Real class," he kept repeating. He would emphasize his remarks by grabbing, from time to time, for his girl friend's crotch. Impassive, she continued driving. She did not even turn her head. "Real class," he went on. "She sees a man for what he is. She takes me for what I am." He reached for his girl again. "Not," he said, staring dreamily out of the window, "like these middle-class cunts." He rambled on until we were on the hill to our house, when, in a kind of *extase*, he began to slap his girl friend's face. With his open palm he slapped the left side of her face, and with the back of his hand the right. His girl just drove, as though this were windshield wipers, or some other feature of the jeep. "Wasn't that something, luv?" Hendon kept saying. Class.

"I can't believe it," people said, almost with passion. It was that year's version of hello. "I can't believe it," people said, on the beach, on the slopes, in hotel lobbies, in cells, at parties. Apparently incredulous, astounded, people met. Sometimes the rejoinder was "For God's sake," as in "Harry! Maude! I can't believe it." "Marilyn! Well, for God's sake." Sometimes people changed it slightly. When we had just come back to the office, a middle-aged couple, he with the heartiness of another era, she with a certain trembly superstition, met in the elevator only yesterday. "Well, as I live and breathe," he shouted. "Touch wood," she replied.

WHAT WAR

The Surveyor moon shot was, in many ways, the best, a coltish tripod on its spindly legs; the first shot it transmitted back to earth was a shy little photo of the shadow of its foot. The Russian instrument had been, by contrast, stolid, plump; it sat up there. We were not told what photographs it sent. The second thing Surveyor did was to use its little shovel, and to send back information about what it dug. It kept sending photographs, of its foot, of its other feet, of its own long, thin shadow on the moon. After some weeks, its batteries expired. It had been useful. It was written off as dead. A few weeks later, sunwarmed, it suddenly began to transmit again. Taking those photographs of its shadows and its feet, like a tourist posed, bashful and proud, on its lunar monument. Then, it again expired. But when, some weeks later, Surveyor II was sent up, Surveyor I woke up yet again. They would both transmit. For weeks and months, they would wake up, drowse, wake up, transmit. They were frail and gangling, but they frolicked quite a long time on the moon.

And, right after the first man landed and walked upon the moon, there was a television program in which a reporter for a network interviewed small children in their school about their views of the event. He asked various questions and received various answers, straightforward or coy. When he asked his last question, what was the moon made of, he heard from the smug children, about green cheese. Some said the moon was made of paper, two said neon light. A vote was taken. The green-cheese children, in their nyah nyah voices, seemed to have chanted everybody down. There remained one unconvinced, iconoclastic child. The moon, she said, in a sensible, lofty tone of pure conviction, is made of grabbedy.

"Now, we'll keep our chin straps down, and the mouthpiece in the mouth," the coach said to the ten-year-olds, in their expensive uniforms, preparing to play football. "Anybody sees wishbone formation, he yells 'Wishbone!' Don't look at them," he said, nodding toward the other team, which was from a larger town and looked a little older. "They're bigger than us, some of them, but they're leery of us and they're thinking. Now, we'll do our huddle, say our Hail Mary, and then," he said, "we'll get them." It is true that we all grew up in a gentler spirit than that might reflect. It is also true that we are all here now, in our city lives, and our city jobs, and nobody came and got us for them in our bassinets.

Later, years later, when nobody was thinking of the moon, the orphans from Vietnam arrived. To a baby, presumably, being picked up by giants and put down in one place seems no more arbitrary than being picked up by other giants and put down in another place entirely. Here they were. A family named Cavanaugh or something was being interviewed about its newest member, the infant Kim Su Cavanaugh, who was already fast asleep beside her teddy bear. The adult Cavanaughs, particularly Mrs. Cavanaugh, kept burbling about how happy they were. Asked how she felt, Mrs. Cavanaugh said happy, many times. Then the Cavanaugh children were interviewed. The youngest Cavanaugh, a seven-year-old, who looked particularly miserable and embittered, was asked how she felt to have a baby sister now. "Happy," she said. The reporter asked whether there was anything she hoped to do with her baby sister. Her face became frightening. In what was still a baby voice, she said "No." The reporter, happily insistent, asked whether there was anything she would like to *teach* her baby sister. The face contorted with thought for a moment; then she said, in her baby voice, very slowly, "Monopoly."

I am normally the sort of reporter who hangs around, or rather, tags along. I have never been any good at interviews. The first man I was ever sent to interview was an English actor, middle-aged, successful, easy, talkative. I went, with my notebook, to see him backstage after his play, which was a hit. I was introduced to him. He said Hello. I said Hello, how are you? It was the last question I could think of to ask. He managed to talk for quite some time. He said he was fine. He went on with an anecdote, in a little monologue. When he came to a pause and seemed about to falter, I tried repeating the last few words he had said, with a little interrogative inflection at the end. "Little interrogative inflection at the end?" I would say, if he had just said that. That worked all right. I would repeat what he'd said, as a question. Yes, he would say, and start out on another little monologue. He was not a reticent or a shy man. A boring man, in a way, but not at all shy. In the end, I was getting him down. Only a half-hour had passed. The actor's words were slowing, limping; one could hear his verbal engine cough. He smiled. He started up again. "You know," he said, heartily, "I'm very

eager to get back to England." Pause. "To see my two sons."
He looked at me, encouragingly. I tried. "You have two
sons?" I said. "Yes," he said. He was not going any further.
I tried again. I tried to look moved. I scribbled in my notebook. "Two," I said. "Sons." He said, "Tell me, Miss Fain.
Are you a professional reporter?" Well, I am. I'm the sort
who tags along, that's all.

Mattie Stokes, who is black and from Trinidad, grew up
in Rochester and was sent through college by Xerox. She
became a systems analyst, taught nights at the New School,
and was the assistant to a radical Fordham dean. She was
living in Bedford-Stuyvesant when I first went to see her. I
was writing about blacks in the city universities. There were
hardly any. Mattie's rooms were in an elegant townhouse of
the sort that still exists in the middle of Brooklyn's hardest
criminal warrens. It was cold. The landlord was trying to
drive the tenants out. Ninety slum tenants in a given space
at the going rate per yard is more profitable than twelve
bourgeois tenants, even at high rents. So it was cold. The
radiators were off, the hot water was off, the boiler was off.
Everything was off. Friends kept wandering into Mattie's
apartment to talk about legal matters. Everyone was drinking beer. I drank beer. I tried to look as though I knew what
I was doing there. "Are you here for an interview," Mattie
finally said, "or are you going to sit there like death on a soda
cracker?" We became friends, of course.

The reporter had arrived at the catastrophe without his
notebook. He wrote down everything he could on the backs
of blank checks. Long after midnight, when he had finished
phoning in his story, he stopped, on his way home, at the
neighborhood liquor store. He bought Scotch. He asked the
clerk, who knew him well, to add on ten dollars cash; he
made out his check for the total. "My, my, what's this?" the
clerk said, as he started to put the check in the cash register.
"I can't cash this check. There's endorsements or something

all over the back." The reporter mumbled wearily that they were story notes, that they were on the backs of all his checks that night. "Gosh," the clerk said, when he had gotten the check approved by the owner of the liquor store. The owner added, "You must have been in a poetic mood."

Mattie was married in those days to a man who was, in effect, her brother-in-law. Mattie's youngest sister, who worked in Manhattan, was still a citizen of Trinidad. She had met a Jamaican newspaper reporter. They wanted to marry. Mattie was a U.S. citizen. She married him. He went straight from the wedding to live with Mattie's sister, which was the idea. Some months after I met Mattie, this brother-in-law became a fugitive from justice. This husband, really, since they had never bothered to divorce. Mattie was by this time planning to be seriously married, to the lawyer who took over her building's tenants' case. There she was, married to a fugitive from justice. Within weeks, he was on the F.B.I.'s Most Wanted List. Mattie pretended to be bitterly pleased by this development. If the F.B.I. managed to find him, she would be able to find him, to arrange for divorce. Everyone who had known him had thought of him, anyway, as married to Mattie's sister. The sister hadn't liked him or seen him in years.

A problem with the F.B.I.'s Most Wanted List, however, is that, like the Bureau itself, it is designed to trace criminals who look a certain way. A glower, a scar, a tattoo, a maniacal stare, but a plain white male criminal way. When it comes to blacks, or to white students gone underground from campuses, the Bureau just can't find them, or, more specifically, can't tell them apart. Can't tell the blacks apart. Can't tell the loose, straight-haired college girls apart. It is a source of great embarrassment. Finding Dohrn, Alpert, Boudin, or even Hearst, when other people are constantly seeing them, is just not what these men are good at. Only last week, the Bureau announced that one of those fugitive girls might be "feigning pregnancy." It struck me as a strange idea of what constitutes disguise. Whiskers, I would have thought, yes. Sunglasses even, a wig; but pregnancy, no. Jim says I misunderstood what the Bureau meant. The "feigned pregnancy" was considered, not as a disguise, but as a means of getting people not to shoot. I don't know. Anyway, though they did find those California fugitives, in their purple jogging shorts, Mattie's brother-in-law, so far as is known, has not even been seen.

Seven years ago, I bought a rifle. When I took it home from the sporting-goods store, I found in the box, not the fully assembled thing, which I had weighed, and tested, and shot, but two pieces—one, almost the whole rifle; the other, a little firing mechanism that had to be attached to it. There was also a little pamphlet, with a half page of instructions for putting the rifle together, six pages of instructions for joining the National Rifle Association. I could have figured out how to join the N.R.A. without those instructions, particularly since the pamphlet included an application for membership. But I could not, no matter how slowly or how often I read that first half page, or at what hour of the day, understand how to attach the firing mechanism to the other part. Anyone can do it. Any child who hunts squirrel, any hunter who cannot read without running his finger along under the words, any psychotic halfwit who wants to shoot some stranger through the head. I could not fathom the problem in any way.

I finally put the rifle, both parts, under a couch, where they gathered dust for years. One winter night, when the gas and electricity had been blown out of service by the wind, a man from the power company came by to restore light and heat. I waited, in the dark, while he did his job. When the lights were on, I mentioned the rifle. I said I'd forgotten how to assemble it. He asked to see it. I brought it out. He squinted down the barrel and, with a single motion, clicked the second part in place. I use that rifle often now. I have always liked to shoot—not living things, but targets, and matchboxes and cans. But putting the damn thing together was and, I guess, always will be one of those simple operations of life that seem to complicate themselves altogether out of my range.

Three of us used to take tennis lessons at the armory at eight-thirty every weekday morning. The light from the dusty bulbs was yellow and bad. The courts consisted of creaky floorboards overlaid with a thin sheet of rubber, which was cracked and patched with tape. We three first met, through our lessons, in September. We all played each day, with a crash-program fanaticism. For months, the instructors had pointed out that we would all save money if we gave up our separate lessons. We all refused. Jane even played on weekends at the armory. Fran stayed home with her kids. On weekends, I simply moved my eight-thirty lessons out to the country. I played with Stewart, who is the coach out there. He started to take me to see professional tennis matches, sometimes to a movie, once to a concert by the local piano teacher, who would have had a grand career but for his nerves. By summer, there were four mornings of tennis lessons with Stewart, four evenings for going to see movies or just driving around. He had a mustache and a beard, and gruff good manners. He was thirty-two. He wanted to work for mankind. He wanted to teach children. He felt bohemian stirrings. Altogether a good, confused man. On the courts, he never shouted, almost never spoke. None of the "Racket back," "Watch the ball," "Run, run, run" that drives one to distraction, although some people do not seem to mind. Once, at the armory, I heard the coach shout incessantly, for a solid hour, at the mayor. The most Stewart would say on the court was, every third lesson or so, an almost inaudible "Backhand." He would slam the ball to the forehand side. That was his little joke. Once in a while, he said "Nice shot." I used to say thanks, or mutter. Then, Stewart said the proper thing to say was nothing, or at most, un huh. So I said un huh. For the rest, he just kept hitting the ball to the outer limit of his students' ability to return it.

122

They were run ragged. Their tennis improved. I have been wrong about a lot of things. I still have his tie.

In the bar of his father's hotel, with the leather chairs that give one the feeling of sitting in a wallet, Dommy has introduced a new drink, Last Mango in Paris. A steep decline.

Of the four baby birds in the barn, three had learned to fly and one stood on the floor, looking stupid and making flapping motions. Now and then, it would walk out in the driveway, where it was dive-bombed by its siblings and snapped at by its parents. Then it would walk back into the barn again. The people in the house checked under the wheels of their cars to avoid running over this bird, and otherwise wished it well. On the third day, the children minced a worm and tried to feed the bird themselves. By the fourth day, one adult or another, thinking himself unwatched, would lean over the bird and mutter, and flap his arms in what he hoped was an exemplary way. On the fifth day, the bird was sitting on a high rafter of the barn with the rest of its family. It has not yet been seen to fly. Perhaps it walked up there.

Like most lonely women, like most women of all kinds, Margaret Dageman had an imaginary lover, with whom she entered the conversation and even the gossip of her friends. I used to think this sort of lover was specific to girls or women who were left out. An imaginary lover explained it. He was married. He was in Korea. He was married and in Korea. He was not married or in Korea, he was nearby, but he worked odd hours. He was not nearby, he was at the end of some line where a train must be taken. Wherever he was, he was not placed to appear or to walk them to the door. I used to think it was only lonely women who, according to temperament, flatly said, or shyly intimated, or just insisted that they had, in fact, this lover, this escort, this beau, this young man, this fiancé, whatever they called him, whom social necessity had obliged them to invent. But it is not so.

It is not so. Most women have had them, at some time in their lives, or all their lives. And I do not mean the private man of daydreams or psychoanalytic literature. It is of the nature of this invented lover that his existence be a matter of public knowledge and, with luck, belief. If a woman were able to manage her own news to perfection, he would be thought to be her profoundest secret, the steady center of her emotional life.

I have known a woman's own husband to be the central character in such a fantasy; quite often, in the lives of intelligent or wordly women, the man himself is real. Quite often too, like most thoughts and suspicions, the fantasy has truth in it; the invention may be reciprocal, or shared. In fact, the only thing this secret lover has in common with any classic rape fantasy is this: that it important that this story seem to come out in spite of a woman's reticence and discretion, against her will. This leads to any number of false confidences, any number of lies told in the false confessional mode. It is a way for a romantic temperament to generate its story line, its lifelong plot. He may be elusive. He may be importunate. He may be neither, or both. He can be anything. The major difference between Margaret Dageman's imaginary lover and anybody else's was only that she engaged in a bitter, an epic quarrel with him.

The mangy dog in the hallway had a grieving look and a furrowed brow. He had been picked up in the street by a lady who attracts animals. Once, a large, rare bird had flown directly from the zoo, on the board of which the lady was, and perched on the lady's window sill. She called the zoo. The keepers had just noticed at that moment that the bird was gone. They came with a large and elaborate net to pick up the bird. The whole incident came to be regarded as an uncanny moment in the zoo's and the lady's history. Anyway, she had now attracted this mangy dog. He was not full-grown. The lady's own dog, shiny, adult, well-fed, had an affronted look. I offered to take the stray. I regretted the offer the next morning. If people were always to cancel on the basis of the next day's regrets, no contracts would go through. Three days later, the lady and both dogs arrived at our brownstone. When they got to the living room, they all sat down. "Now, think pleasant thoughts, Luke," she said to the grieving dog. "We named him Luke," she said to me. "Don't you think he looks like a Luke? We have tried to get him to think pleasant thoughts. You must remember to medicate his ears." Luke moved in. Ben, our photo editor from Georgia, said Luke looked like what is called a coon hound in the South. The great lady philosopher said, "Now, never mind. That's an authentic dog." Within a month of Luke's arrival, and during the convalescence of his ears, he moved next door. I don't know how he managed it. The designer who owns that house already had two Afghan hounds. He's happy there. "Beards within beards," the designer sometimes says of city life. "Well, never mind."

Joel Seidington thought when he knew what a thing was called, he had it nailed. Or rather, a thing burned more brightly for a second when he held its name to it; then it was ash. Joel thought, in particular, that he understood other people's pleasures when he had found the word for them. That's a tango, he would say, with considerable satisfaction, to the girl he had brought to sit beside him at a prom or, years later, in a night club. That's a lindy, now, and there's a waltz. They would sit. He would smile. They would watch. He would name what went by. It was the same in Joel's work, and in everything else with which he had to do. An elegant exposition, Joel would say, when one of his colleagues in the chemistry department had just set forth a breakthrough in a lifetime's experiment. Or, Al has just birdied the sixth, that's an inside straight Tim is holding, Martin's daughter has taken up dressage. That's the B-minor Mass, that's a fado, they've been raising black angus, they're called collard greens, actually, Kate and Martin still seem enamored of each other, don't you think. This insistence on calling things something had little to do with true pedantry, an obsession for getting things right. Almost any formulation would suit him. It was a more primitive instinct, in some ways—as though to name a thing were to cut its nails and hair, and pocket them, and put the adversary in his power. In another way, the instinct was entirely modern: to impress on everything that passed his way Joel's word for it, his personal bureaucratic rubber stamp.

Edith Piaf was in one of her many, absolutely last concerts at the Paris Olympia. She was singing "Je ne suis pas folle." She ended the song, as always, with maniac laughter. On this particular evening, someone way back in the theater echoed that laughter. At first, it was thought to be a prankster, or at least a heckler. Then it was thought to be part of the performance. But when that insane laugh continued, bitter, chilling, on Edith Piaf's precise note, like one tuning fork of madness responding to another, three ushers and six members of the audience escorted the laughing lady, with infinite courtesy, to the street.

Joel was the only man I ever knew whose car had a seat belt on only one side, his. There was something about him that made it unthinkable to laugh, or even to dislike him after all. In my first year of graduate school, I found myself, for instance, in Joel's car, for what he called a rallye at his motor club. Whatever I thought he meant, it never occurred to me that Joel was going to drive in it. The race turned out to be as much for mileage as for speed. Fifteen points on the map were to be driven to in any order. The car that reached all fifteen points the fastest was to be one sort of winner. The other winner would be the car that reached them all by travelling the fewest miles. At the end, the judges would decide between these winners for the trophy. I did not understand what other standards would apply. Also, I cannot read maps; my sense of direction is so poor and unstable that maps somehow make it worse. They bring on confusions not only of east-west, north-south, but also of left and right. Joel, who had no way of knowing that, explained the race to me, told me to navigate, handed me the map, fastened his seat belt, and drove. We never saw any of the other cars again. We reached the first point in three hours, the second never. All through the afternoon and into the evening, Joel, pale, would say to me, from time to time, in a flat, strained voice, which had its gallantry, "It's all right. I'm not competitive."

We went skiing. We had not gone in years. We drove for hours through a blizzard, in the car of the natural athletes —jumpers on trampolines on Mondays, squash players and ice skaters on other week nights, and just to top the note of general health, players of string quartets on Thursday afternoons. The athletes were impatient with the snow that slowed the driving. They approached a cliff en route and climbed it, in an interim show of fitness. We barely followed. It was ice. Then the athletes whooped, dived and slid headfirst down the cliff. It was steep. The athletes seemed invigorated. They drove on. When they reached the ski hut, everybody put on snowshoes. After ten steps, I thought I might not make it. Skiing was worse. With great effort, I maintained a slow and trembling snowplow recalled from childhood, side to side, graceless, across the mountain, worried by passing schussers, cold. "It won't hurt you, you know," one of the athletes said, as though he were imparting useful information, "to point your skis downhill."

Downhill. One of the President's closest friends was interviewed, at length, on television. He repeatedly spoke of the President as a witty man. He stressed the wonderful sense of humor of this President. The interviewer asked him for an example. The President's friend demurred. The interviewer suggested that the friend could surely think of one instance of it. The friend, beginning to smile, declined. The interviewer pressed for just a single example, just one remembered time. The President's friend was beginning to suppress what was obviously great mirth, as he started on this anecdote:

The President, and this friend, and another friend were on an island. "And we had," the friend said, "this pair of rubber legs, you know?" He said this as though everyone had a pair of rubber legs. "This pair of woman's rubber legs. And a wig, you know." His amusement and anticipation were such by now that he could hardly hold his laughter back. "And the President, the President suggested that we put them"—here a laugh—"in the bed. So we put the wig on the pillow, and a blanket, you know, with just the rubber legs sticking out" —from here on, the laughter began to escape control—"and he told me to hide behind the curtain, so when Bob came in" —by now, he was laughing so hard he had to pause—"I was hiding behind the curtain. And he showed Bob the bedroom, and the bed had the wig and those rubber legs, you know. The President didn't say anything about it. And Bob, well, I thought Bob was going to . . ." That was it. It was not just his laughter that indicated the anecdote was over. It was clear that, whatever he had thought Bob was going to, the President's friend's account of the President's sense of humor seemed to him complete. Well, I voted for him. Not twice, but once. I did vote for him. I don't see any reason why a President should be a witty man, or a man responsible for the assumptions of his closest friends about his wit. He's out, as Manuel said, "Mr. Nixon has go out." He's not at his desk. He's in a meeting. We worked for that, too. And that sort of anecdote doesn't come into it at all. It was just the exoticism I was not prepared for. The most natural thing in the world, a pair of rubber legs.

A tall man was beginning a Tiny Tim sort of grateful frenzy—covering his ears, and shaking his head and saying, shrilly, often, how wonderful to him everybody was, how wonderful. Once, at a Christmas party on Park Avenue, when somebody was reading, beautifully, aloud from Dickens, I began to giggle, uncontrollably. It was that classic Tiny Tim and his damn crutch. I have always thought of the

128

other, singing Tiny Tim as serious. Elva Miller, Frances Foster Jenkins, but Tiny Tim especially—being somehow *bent* to play out the American freak triumphant, to sing in falsetto about tulips, when what he longs to do, knows how to do, does seriously, is sing in exact imitation of 78 r.p.m. records, complete with scratches, old forgotten songs, in exact imitation of the voices of the dead. There he was, then, Tiny Tim, on the talk shows, in no sense a comedian but a loser meant to win it for the losers. The underside, a fifties person. Or rather, contra-fifties, in his peculiar way. For years now, there have been other, sounder contra-fifties people. Against all that modesty, domestication, niceness—Joe Namath, Bobby Fischer, Mark Spitz, Jimmy Connors, Bobby Riggs, Muhammad Ali. For the ladies, well, for the ladies, Marilyn Monroe, Sylvia Plath, Diane Arbus, Janis Joplin, Anne Sexton, and, after all on another racetrack, Ruffian.

All those unendearing braggarts and, on the distaff side, the suicides. Books about Ali. Ten years earlier, the preoccupation with Monroe. But there was a day, or there came, as Sam Dash would say, a time, when an actual Evel Knievel metaphor appeared—in an event that was inconsequential, small. The proposition was deep. It virtually spun. People were invited to see somebody ride his motorcycle over a canyon gap. That was what it was said they had been invited to pay to see. An early truth of the matter was this: it could not be done. The performer and his sponsors knew what he was going to do. The people who paid their admission knew what they were coming to see. By the end, the morally spinning proposition was this: when, by some miscalculation, the motorcyclist was actually exposed to a danger which he had not foreseen, when his parachutes almost failed so that he nearly did get killed (not, it is true, in a manner that had anything to do with the alleged hazards of his ride, but rather by being slammed by his parachutes into the sides of cliffs), when, in short, the escape procedure became the menace, were the members of the audience entitled to feel cheated in any way. They had paid to see him die. He had arranged to escape unharmed. There was nothing of the old-style prestidigitator-understanding in this thing. In their separate ways, neither party ever seriously entertained any notion that the motorcycle could rocket successfully over that canyon gap. What did, then, occur; what was the event? A performer and an audience conspired that someone should be misled. The performer intended a motorized parachute jump. The audience paid to see a suicide. No fifties teamwork or nice-guy qualities in it anywhere. Nothing went according to plan. The question was who was misled, whom were they conspiring to mislead? Why, history. For a perfect moment it was like almost every other event in public life.

On the shuttle from Washington to New York, I started to take a seat in the first row. All passengers except the few who think that, in case of a crash, the tail section will be spared try to sit in forward rows, in order to save time in getting off. A stewardess said the first three rows on this flight were reserved. We all, resignedly, moved further back. One meek-looking man, however, balked, protested, said that this time they had gone too far. He knew, he said, they knew, everyone knew that federal law forbids reserving seats on shuttle flights. He would insist, he would notify, he would denounce. In fact, under the rule of first come first served, he would sit down. A stewardess, meanwhile, was gently herding him to the fourth row. A steward, looking young, and blond and fit, said the seats had been reserved for reasons of security. The ranting man demanded to know for whom. The steward said, for reasons of security, he could not tell their names. The rant had subsided to a grumble that passengers had at least a right, a perfect right to know the names of any celebrities they were being put through this absurd outrage for, when a group came aboard and sat down in those seats. Among them, laughing, with a black patch across his eye, was a passenger who would cause any other passenger in the world to recognize a problem of security.

An extremely old, infirm and doddering lady, carrying an enormous bag, part wicker and part canvas, had meanwhile quietly taken an aisle seat in the first row. She sat, staring straight ahead and trembling, apparently unaware that her presence was now the subject of discussion, in at least two languages, throughout the plane. A man in the new group, who was himself carrying a large canvas parcel, whispered a while with two men in the third row and then approached the lady, with the evident intention of asking her to move. He stopped, shaking his head. He couldn't do it. He walked back, to a seat in the fourth row. Passengers of all sorts and races were still coming aboard. The whole aircraft scrutinized them, for evidences of fanaticism.

The steward, a stewardess and the co-pilot were now whispering. Just before takeoff, when the plane was full, the stewardess bent over the old lady, trying to get her to part, at least, with that enormous bag. The lady sat, at first, not hearing, trembling. Then she said, "My crackers, inside. I am going to want." As the plane started down the runway, the lady rummaged and found her crackers. The bag was examined, discreetly, and put away. We took off. Halfway to New York, she ate her crackers. Then, surprisingly, she got up and began to wander toward the rear. After a few steps, she went back to her seat, beckoned to a stewardess, and began to mumble for a while. The stewardess elicited the information that the lady's son was a famous journalist, that she had recognized the renowned man in the seat behind her, that her son would not believe that she had been on the same flight with such a person, that her best friend, who was in any case at times these days quite senile, would not believe it either, that in sum she would like that man's autograph. There were consultations. Then she got it. Then she had no place to put it. She required her bag. There was another ripple of apprehension that she might be, after all, the world's most improbable terrorist, with a weapon hidden, after all, in that enormous bag. She spent the rest of the flight, though, staring, doddering, holding on to the bag by its string.

The sign that Manley Dubois had entered a woman's life might be her collection of Billie Holiday records. Women confided in Manley Dubois. They described him as the only man they could trust. There is a high edge of ill temper in vain women which no other women and, among men, only a self-parodying category of homosexuals permit themselves. The edge is common in women who have been beautiful since birth, or think they have; it also exists in women of power in the arts. Such women—and extremely gentle women—have confidences. Everyone has secrets. Most women have shames or sins or crimes. But confidences, apart from the lives of schoolgirls, belong to women of timidity or power. It was these that Manley encouraged to share their grief, their blues, their sense of life and earth, with him, through any singer one could love. At lunch, or of an evening *à deux,* in that tipsy intimacy which was his special note, Manley often comforted the woman who was confiding in him at the moment with the secrets of the woman who had confided in him the evening before. Dubois was a writer, who had played a great part in the creation of the particular society in which he moved. People in a confessional frame of mind rarely drew the obvious inference. Or perhaps they simply would not be deterred. When he finally came to write about it, it turned out, strangely, that he had never understood his material at all.

One night last week, a lady from public broadcasting called. I had been watching *Medical Center.* A girl who would require open heart surgery was in love with a young man who had just had his appendix removed. He was retarded. He was in love with her, too, over the objections of his sister, who was possessive about him and hurt his feelings a lot. The lady from public broadcasting asked whether I would like to take part in a symposium on Politics and the Media. I said I couldn't. She asked where she could reach Jim. I said I thought at the office. She asked whether I thought Jim would like to participate in a symposium on Law and the Media. I said I didn't know. Then, she said, "Hey. Are you watching *Medical Center*?" I said I was. It turned out she had been watching it too. We talked awhile longer. She asked if I ever listened to radio. I said I did. "Well," she said, "after we finish our marathon reading of Trollope and Proust, we're going to move right into the Federalist Papers." She laughed. She asked whether I would like to participate in a symposium they were having on the female orgasm in fiction. I said, thanks but no. She asked if I could suggest somebody. They had five people; they needed one more. I said I couldn't think of anybody. Could I suggest any novels, though, besides the ones they had already thought of. I said I couldn't think of any besides the ones they must have thought of, *Ulysses,* D.H. Lawrence. She said, And Mrs. Dalloway. I said, Mrs. *Dall*oway?

For weeks, I had been stalking the prowler. He stood, late most nights, just inside the glass outer door of the house, in the hallway, fumbling with the doorknob of the secondhand dress shop, which is on our ground floor. He just stood there, fumbling and smoking many cigarettes. I could see him from the sidewalk. When he saw me, he would leave, brushing by me and muttering. At other times, when he didn't notice me, I would watch him. Some nights, I thought of locking the glass outer door while he was in there, and holding it locked until someone came and caught him; I could not quite imagine, though, how that would end. Last month, I really did catch him. I had been out to dinner, which I left early, in order not to get drunk. It was on Fifth Avenue. I found a cab. An elderly gentleman, who had left the dinner too, got in beside me. He said it was not safe, after dark in this city, for a lady to take a cab home alone. He dropped me at my door. He said we ought to have lunch, please to call him. He went off in the cab, not having noticed the prowler inside the glass door. I hadn't noticed him either, until then. The prowler, smoking, fumbling, didn't notice me at all.

I walked a few steps away along the sidewalk. There was nobody else around except one young, cheerful man walking toward me. "Excuse me," I said. "I live two houses from here. There's a prowler inside the doorway, in the hall." The young man walked back. He looked in through the glass door. "I see there is," he said. "I'll walk you in if you like. If he isn't armed, I can take him." I said, No, thanks. "I practically know him. This time I'd like to call the police. I'll try that pay phone at the corner." He said, "I'll walk you over. Just dial 911. 411's information. I'll walk on this side." We passed a few people on the way to the corner. The man walking with me suddenly shouted, "Phil. Hey, Phil. Nice to see you." He shook the hand of a bearded man who had just crossed the street. They were delighted to have met. Another friend of Phil's crossed the street then. There were introductions. Phil offered me a dime for the pay phone. I used it. I called the police. I gave Phil his dime back. We shook hands. They went off. My original friend had gone back to stand outside the glass door of my building. When a police car pulled up, he said, "Goodbye. Take care." I said, "Thanks." He went away. More squad cars arrived. Two policemen went into the building. Another squad car. I was now standing with six policemen at the curb. A slightly drunk, kind and friendly-looking man walked to us, and asked whether I was all right and whether I had a boyfriend. I said I had. He said, "Sure?" I said, "Absolutely." I pointed to one of the policemen. "O.K., sweetheart," the drunk man said, and walked away. It occurred to me, and I am almost certain, that he thought he was coming to the aid of someone alone, being arrested by six men in uniform, when, after all, it was I who called the police.

Somebody was nudging my tray along the rail at the museum cafeteria. I was trying to keep my tray from bumping the tray ahead. I held my fingers firmly on the tray top, hooked my thumbs underneath the steel bar. The pressure of the nudging tray increased. I gave in to the superior determination. Doubtless, the tray pusher had had an awful day. I let go. My tray slid into the next tray, which slid into the next, which crashed into another. At the cashier's corner, there was a pileup. Tea bags, jello, trays all over everything.

Our defense correspondent used to be so well informed that his pieces made only ordinary sense to readers of the paper; to members of what is called the intelligence community they made such perfect sense that agencies and weapons analysts did not simply wonder what he might be up to; they were scared. It was not at all clear what they were going to do about it. They themselves did not expect to be done away with at the end of their working days or even to enter anonymous retirement; they expected to write thrillers during their careers and memoirs after. But they could not believe, on the basis of his columns, that the over-informed correspondent, far from being any sort of clandestine professional, was that rarity, a truly industrious reporter, doing a thorough job. Our editors didn't understand it, either. He was, finally, transferred away from defense matters. The correspondent, a modest man and a steady drinker, thought his transfer had to do with some deficiency in his writing style. He already admired what were widely thought to be the great reporters. His early, happiest days in journalism had been as a reporter for his father's failing rural paper. He had written a regular column called "Wanderings in Rural Penn." His first report had concerned an oak tree, which appeared to have the largest girth of any in Penn County. Immediately, he had received letters from county readers who claimed to have seen wider local oaks. He had gone to measure; he had been fair. He had written columns about the largest egg yolk in the county, and the smallest, and the egg that contained the largest number of yolks. He had traveled around the county, solemnly breaking eggs to make certain just how many yolks they did contain. His column had inspired, always, a brisk and concerned correspondence. The paper's circulation improved. His father raised his salary. Those were his best years. When, so many years later, he was transferred to the culture desk, he knew that he was through.

It certainly does not do to have too low a threshold for being insulted. Even the affectionate insult, or the compliment with any sort of spin on it, can reverberate in memory in awful ways. "I love your little fat legs," Paul said to Joanne. He had watched her walking toward him on the beach. He was so in love with her that, although he meant it, he may not even have heard what he said, exactly. She never forgave him. She slept with him for another year and then married his enemy and rival, the only man Paul had ever hated in the world. "You have beautiful eyes and lovely hands," Leroy said to Jane, "and when you smile, to me you're beautiful." She never forgave him, either. She married him. Their life together was hell for fifty years. "Has anyone ever told you that you're lovely?" is, of necessity, a minefield. There is no conceivable proper answer. It all ends in disaster anyway.

The lady was not just a vegetarian; she had many theories, about food, and the elements around one, about smells. The smell of x-rays, the smell of diets of one sort and another. She spoke a lot of the *va et viens* of the elements, and the foods one ate. She pointed out she had heard that we smell badly to the Japanese. She interrupted her discourse for a moment, paused, and then turned to the sculptor beside her. "Do we smell badly to you, Mr. Omura?" she said.

Contrary to the lore of restaurants and hotel schools, I find the women I know do tip reasonably and drink a lot. They are all educated women, though—in that age group which learned its courtesies from its own mothers; its loves from Paolo and Francesca, Brontë, Joyce, and even O'Hara; and all the solid enthusiasms in its cast of mind from what we used to emphasize were not anthologies, textbooks, or other secondary works, but from originals, the works themselves. Our ambitions were, nonetheless, what those of any sensible group of women at that time, perhaps at any modern time, ought to have been: to become safe and successful; to marry someone safe and successful; to have for our children some sort of worldly safety and success. From time to time, however, there is something, I don't know, wistful, about how it has turned out. Not just Brecht's great ship of the eight sails and the fifty cannon. The other ships. Perhaps the tall ships, the fleet, the craft, the other ships that don't come in.

It is not at all self-evident what boredom is. It implies, for example, an idea of duration. It would be crazy to say, For three seconds there, I was bored. It implies indifference but, at the same time, requires a degree of attention. One cannot properly be said to be bored by anything one has not noticed, or in a coma, or asleep. But this I know, or think I know, that idle people are often bored and bored people, unless they sleep a lot, are cruel. It is no accident that boredom and cruelty are great preoccupations in our time. They flourish in a single region of the mind. Embarrassment, though, on the scale of things to feel, is trivial. It does not even constitute —as do humiliation, envy, guilt—an actual emotion, a condition of the soul. Its command of the attention is absolute. Someone who needs and does not have a handkerchief is likely to be as preoccupied as someone scared to death. Most of the safest form in this is established by form, by sameness, rote. For others, the stereotyped is most embarrassing. It is by no means clear on which side of this question humor is. A surprise can be comic, as can a certainty. Leaving humor out of it, there exists embarrassment pure. Alas.

We had ordered martinis, straight up, with a twist of lemon. The waitress had brought martinis with olives. This had the force of an *éclaircissement.* "Not exactly a twist of lemon," I said when she had left. "No," Jim said, "it isn't." That was it. I have known Jim, after all, a long time. I still make these inane attempts to have a conversation. Once, in a call from Natchez, Jim uncharacteristically interrupted a memo he was reading to me, to say, "Hello, are you there?" I could understand what had happened. "Just because I haven't interrupted you," I said, "you think I died."

I have lived alone now, I think, as long as anybody who is not a hermit or a kook or a spinster who keeps cats. Not entirely alone, but mostly—very far from intermittently. Jim, for instance, when he stays here, makes his telephone calls on his credit card. Rarely, somebody has called him here, collect. The last time was months ago. We were asleep. He was on the phone a long time. Jim didn't say much. He hardly ever says much. I wonder what we would ever talk about if there were no news. A lot of people depend on him, really. And Joe, the candidate's deputy, seems to count on us both, separately, without any idea that we even see each other, except through him, Joe. There have been some odd results. Jim, having come in from New Orleans or Chicago, uses his credit card to call his office, where there is always somebody late at night. Message from Joe. Please call. I, having gone to meet Jim at the airport, call my answering service. Message from Joe. Please call. "You first, or me first?" Jim says. "You, I think," I say. Jim fixes drinks and brings them to the bedroom. "Maybe we ought to wait till morning," he says. We consider it. He looks at his watch. He takes out his credit card, sits on the bed, and dials.

The maternity ward was separated from the intensive-care ward by a small corridor in which there was a single pay phone. There were also two waiting rooms, one with a painted shingle reading DADS, the other with a bronze plaque, MEDITATION ROOM. "Dads" had a television set. "Meditation Room" had two burners and a coffee pot. The families of the patients wandered freely between them, for coffee or conversation or, at crowded hours, space. A senile friend of an intensive-care patient kept calling in, at all hours, on the pay phone. He wasn't, it turned out, even a close friend. His persistence and his desperation were such that if we did not pick up the phone and talk to him sometimes, he would call the patient's family or even the nurses in the ward, direct. Since everyone was always bringing chocolates to the nurses in intensive care, the doctors coming out of there were always chewing something.

"Of course I haven't confused you with somebody else. Either it was you, or I made it up."

The operative thing about the parties was that everyone who was asked did actually go to them and that the food and drink were of an awfulness, and also scarcity, that would embarrass New York dropouts in a loft. The food was always served so late that the hard liquor, such as it was, had run out. The dishes that were meant to be hot were never quite as warm as those that were meant to be chilled. There were not only, for the intrepid, no seconds of anything, there was not enough to go around. This meant that everyone—ambassadors, actresses, bishops, fashionable congressmen, writers, professors and civic-minded nuns—pushed, quite violently pushed, in the direction of the food. When the worst was over, the hostesses were, for some reason, always overwhelmed with compliments. They accepted these graciously. Then, they would begin to marvel about how inexpensively it had all been put together, how little bother or money it had cost. They expected the guests to marvel over this with them, and the guests did marvel. All of us.

What we were doing in Washington was working for a House select committee on private and institutional corruption. It changes its name every twelve years or so, but that's what it is. At the staff offices, we had jobs as consultants, on a temporary basis, at a hundred dollars a day. We were paid thirty-five dollars more, for living expenses, on days we were actually down there, plus fares to and from LaGuardia,

O'Hare, or wherever we were from. A pretty town, Washington, not too large. None of us had ever spent much time there before. At dawn, the joggers in sweat suits would be out, whatever the weather, as would the senator and his procurer, in their sports car with the top down; joggers, senator, procurer, all pale and hungover, would wave. On Mondays, Tuesdays and Wednesdays, our people worked straight through the night. Thirteen secretaries, all night, on high stools in a warehouse, assembling notebooks. "Page 32, Statement 28, Tab 28.2," the head secretary would call out, like a croupier. Each secretary, with three notebooks on a high table before her, would put a Xeroxed loose-leaf page from the stacks on the floor beside her in all three. What they worked on then, these secretaries, calmly, cheerfully, with their smoker's laugh and their smoker's cough, were consoles. They sat like E. Power Biggs at their keyboards, typing words that lit up in neon, at each separate console, on a sort of TV screen. People would rush in and dictate changes in the neon paragraphs. When the page on the screen was edited and complete, the secretary would push a button. While she drank coffee, and we all stood there, drinking coffee, too, and watching, the screen would activate the typewriter and the keys would type, one line from left to right, the next from right to left, in alternation to the bottom of the page. For six months, the fact that the machines could type every other line from right to left, thereby saving the time that would be occupied by returning to the left-hand margin, fascinated everybody. When the neon had finished dictating its last line, the secretary would blank it out, erase the machine's memory of it, and begin another page. By shortly after ten A.M., most of the town's pallor is gone. Most committees are in session. The tired, driven bureaucrats of the night have ceded the place anyway to the men who are, at least nominally, in power; and these, communing with their hometowns or with the night officers at the remotest embassies, are busy exercising their prerogatives.

A much more gentle town, Washington, certainly, than

New York, pretty in its flowers and the scale of its houses, although every street in the last years is being torn up. At the fine hotels, the Hay-Adams, the Sheraton, the Madison, people often sleep to the sound of iron scraping stone and jackhammers on macadam, whenever, for some reason, the work goes on in three shifts, overnight. At the cheaper hotels, like the Quality Inn near the station, the hotel doors, the outside doors, after midnight, are actually locked; people have to pound on the glass from the sidewalks to wake the night porters, who let them back into their hotels. Greg's aunt was for years in love with an exiled African leader, who, being Catholic and already married, could not marry her. This tragic aunt had an equally tragic but more enterprising mother, very old, who had been in love with Russia—all of it. At the time of the Revolution, this lady's thought had been for the English governesses of White Russian children. She had actually commandeered a train. With a confidence, for which she could subsequently find no rational grounds, that every English governess would go to her local railroad station and wait there, the lady took that train all across Russia, picking up English governesses, who were in fact waiting, along the way. Greg himself was on a story in Baghdad, at a time of public hangings and of violent, berserk crowds. At the most expensive hotel, rioters had surged through the lobbies and down corridors, screaming for vengeance, or, at least, for death. Rioters pounded on all the bedroom doors. Anyone who answered to the knock was murdered. Anyone who didn't answer, whether out of fear, or sleepiness, or a habit of not answering when no bellboy had been summoned, was left alone. The aspect of a closed door seemed to check the crowd's momentum; it passed on.

"Tic tac toe, two out of three?" the four-year-old said, sitting down beside us. Then he drew five bars across and four bars down. Jim redrew it for him. The boy considered. He said, "I see."

The judge had quite a number of generous impulses. He gave himself full credit for each of them. He did not carry any of them out. As a result, he was often puzzled and aggrieved by the demands the people closest to him seemed to make upon him. Though he would be the last man in the world to ask for thanks, he could not understand why they were, on the whole, so damned ungrateful. His daughter, who was overweight, but for whom he felt considerable affection, seemed actually to fear him. When he found her reading the latest diet book, or doing calorie computations, he would point out to her that she was deluding herself: the problem was that she simply ate too much and exercised too little. When she avoided his eyes and, muttering denials, left the room, he would tell himself that she was at a difficult age. His moral vanity was great. When it was touched, he became dangerous. It is not at all uncommon for someone to arrive at a scene of brutality or injustice and, with a sympathetic murmur or heroic flourish, attack the victim. It happens all the time. It underlies the columns, for example, of Dr. Franzblau. But the particular consequence of his moral vanity was that when he did people an injury, he never forgave them. Never again.

The whole courtroom is filled with judges. Each one presides. Perhaps there will be a defendant today, although we are not sure. Scholars and intellectuals make bad jurors, I believe. Their attention span is short. They get bored with the point. They overvalue the original. A hunting dog is not an intellectual. There is a mystery in lawyers' expressions. False and misleading statements, for instance. Always together. False and misleading. Can't understand what the "misleading" is doing there. It's always there. And I've found, I think, the strongest "or" in language anywhere. It's the lawyers' phrase: as he then well knew or should have known. Well knew or should have known. The strongest or.

Travelers by jet, like subway commuters, tend to arrive on board at the exact last minute. Intercity bus riders take their seats with lots of time to spare. I was the last, in fact the only, passenger on a special late-night bus from Miami to Key Biscayne. "Sister, be calm," the driver said, as he drove through the darkness. "Jesus is up front here, with me." One of those, I thought. The ride from Miami Beach to Key Biscayne has a drawbridge in it. The ride is long. "Are you nervous?" the driver went on. "You must be from New York." I said nothing. He said, "Yes." I said, "Yes." A long silence. He repeated, "Yes." He suddenly turned in his seat and offered me a battered red book. "Turn to page 324," he said. There seemed no reason not to. I took the book and turned to page 324. "Read it aloud," he said. What the hell, I thought. It wasn't dark. I read aloud, what might have been a hymn. When the driver said the first few lines along with me, I thought it was because he knew them by heart. But it was clear he was dissatisfied; I was doing something wrong. I started reading lines, and pausing. He would say the next lines, in the pauses. It turned out that we were meant to read responsively. We did that page. I gave him back his book. "Yes," he said. "Yes. I have a glorious future. In this life or in the next, it doesn't matter." Pause. "Yes." He asked why I didn't go to church, or read the Bible, or learn to untamp the spiritual power. "Do you pray?" he asked. I said, sometimes. We drove a long time. "I pray twenty-four hours a day," he said. When we had driven quite a lot further, he said, "Yes." Then his voice fell. "Something tells me," he said, "that we have missed our exit." He turned the bus, crossed the divider and found the way.

"I've been doing tunes. I've been doing melodies. I've gone back to it," the kind composer said. "After doing atonal music for twenty years." I asked him what the equivalent of staleness to the point of witlessness in his field was, or whether, in music, such a thing exists. "Oh, yes," he said. "Pitch fatigue."

THE AGENCY

The boat was old. The food was boiled. The berths were not sound. The passage took more than a week. The class in all cabins, on all decks, was tourist class. On the ninth day out of New York, the night before Cobh, there was, near the engine room, a talent show. A girl from Briarcliff tap-danced to a hymn. Three boys from Tufts played "Aloha-Oe" with forks on water glasses filled to various heights. A couple, returning to Bavaria after twenty years, sang "Du, du liegst mir am Herzen" seven times. A clerk from Albany did imitations, turning his back to the audience to compose his face before each one. A Scoutmaster from Tenafly rode his unicycle around the floor. The Bavarian couple's daughter, having been at first reluctant to perform, sang an operatic German

favorite, which translated, turned out to be "Fritz, Rejoice!
Fritz, Rejoice! Tomorrow We Are Having Celery Salad."
And then an Indian student from McGill, who had boarded
the ship at Montreal, slowly, deliberately wound a turban
around his head. That was it. He did not win the prize—a
pastoral scene in marzipan—but he gave one to think what
talent is. Such an interesting conception of it did not come
my way again until, years later, in a trench in the Sinai, an
Israeli soldier, born in Yemen, chewed up and swallowed a
razor blade to impress Yael Dayan.

That year, a Fulbright to Paris had somehow found his
way to a band of street fighters in Budapest. A Florence
Fulbright had died with a party of tourists he had been
leading through the desert in Libya. The Americans were not
staying put. Students on grants abroad lost permission to
receive their checks by mail. Showing up to be paid kept
them, once a month at least, in place. Back home, a group
of students, driving a car across the country for its owner,
whom they did not know (an agency made the transaction),
sped for hours through the desert. It was nearly sundown.
They had seen no other cars since noon. Then, in the distance, with the setting red sun just behind it, they saw a car,
at the world's edge, coming toward them. They laughed and
kept driving. For several minutes, the two cars raced in their
lanes toward each other. Drivers and passengers began to
smile and wave across the desert. A few more seconds—
laughing, shouting, waving—the two cars collided. There
were twelve occupants in all, and none were dead when it was
over. A seventeen-year-old boy regained consciousness in the
air, caught and sustained by telephone wires. He was too
startled to be scared. He climbed down the telephone pole
rungs calmly. His arm was slightly broken. The others, only
bruised, were scattered along several yards of highway. They
picked themselves up gradually, looked at what remained of
the two cars, shuddered, and sat down together.

The arthritic Chihuahua, with cast, glazed eyes, walked among the plates and glasses on the tablecloth. We were in a restaurant near the Banque de France. Madame Devereux was telling her experiences of the war. She had rolled bandages. She had suffered privations, inconveniences. She had endured reports of the conditions at the front. At first, word of the ghettos in Eastern Europe had caught her sympathies. But then she was appalled. They, she was told on high authority, had stolen all the doorknobs off the ghetto doors, and sold the knobs. They were such salesmen; she had been naïve. But when, as Monsieur Devereux had known they would, they turned around and sold the bandages, Madame could roll no more. She caught our eyes. *"N'est-ce pas, mon petit,"* she said, stroking a tufted bald spot behind her Chihuahua's ear. He wheezed and stretched. A wineglass overturned. *"N'est-ce pas, mon petit, qu'ils allaient trop loin."* It was not one of us who overturned the glass. It was the dog. We were trying so hard. Maybe it was our French we were uncertain of.

We had lined up. We had crossed the Atlantic on a small, old boat of the French line called the *Flandre,* which we called the Flounder—partly for the joke but mainly to avoid in each other's presence that attempt to pronounce the French *r,* which seemed of such importance to us then. We had lined up for the *carte de séjour* and the identity card, for student accreditation and for the certificate of equivalence to our American degrees. Having stood in one line long enough to reach the bureaucrat whose job it was to issue one document, we learned that the prerequisite for it was another. At the end of the line for this other, we learned from its bureaucrat that he could not issue his document without evidence that we had already obtained the first, or a third, perhaps others or both. It was the fall of 1961. French students—and, for all we knew, students of every other nationality—were already burning American flags in the Sorbonne courtyard, on behalf, they said, of Cuba. It was clear they hated us. We stood. We smiled. We had gone abroad with the American smile. We were very serious. Only the least serious of us roamed the streets at night, chanting *"La Paix en Algérie"* with one student crowd, or *"Algérie Française"* with another, until the two groups filled the boulevards, converged, and, with the help of massed policemen swinging weighted capes, rioted. On the same night the Marquis de Cuevas was borne by litter to a performance of ballet at the Opera, where he was strewn with rose petals, Bonbon Wechsler of Santa Barbara, who had already acquired a small Moroccan boyfriend and was chanting with him to improve her French, lost track of the boyfriend, and, being carried along by the demonstration, at its edge, was accidentally pushed through the window of a bookshop on the Rue Bonaparte, where she nearly bled to death among the old, incomplete sets of tarot cards. The complete sets had been bought up by American students of *The Waste Land* right after the war.

"Far from it," the man who cleans up this office after hours keeps muttering to himself. "Far from it. Far from it."

The most important line, the longest and the most embittered, was the line for the student restaurants. Some people stood in it for forty-six straight hours. The restaurant card required that all other cards and documents be in order. Quite often, an American or other foreign student would arrive with his completed file at the desk and be met with the stare, the shrug, and look of perfect insolence which characterizes, everywhere, the bureaucrat who likes his power to obstruct. Many students wept. Most of them persisted, with that flat determination to understand the country and the language which took them in so many different ways. In no other language, for instance—certainly not our own—were we so improbably familiar with the vocabulary of churches, with naves, Flamboyant Gothic arches, apses, capitals, transepts; or with the words of medieval hymns and songs of courtly love. We spoke of the quality of the blue in the stained-glass windows of Chartres, which modern science had not been able to reproduce, as though the medieval craftsman who had produced it were a colleague. He had, we knew, billed his diocese for the purchase of sapphires ground up to create that color. Modern science had, at least, established that sapphires played no part in its composition at all. It was our first, most scholarly appreciation of the padded expense account.

The fashion models walked down the ramp, surveyed the audience with utter, unamused contempt, turned, sauntered out. For some reason, this induced the lady customers to buy. Within a year, convinced of many European things and yet unalterably American, we all went home.

We are thirty-five. Some of us are gray. We all do situps or something to keep fit. I myself wear bifocals. Since I am not yet used to wearing specs at all, I tend to underestimate the distance required, for instance, for kisses on the cheek. If the other person wears glasses, too, we are likely to have a brushing clack of frames. We have had some drunks, an occasional psychotic break, eleven divorces, one autistic child, six abortions, two unanticipated homosexuals, several affairs of the sort that are lifelong and quiet and sad, one drowning, two cases of serious illness, one hatred each, no crimes. No crimes is no small thing. We might have run over somebody in high school and left the scene. Before that, we might have stopped putting pennies on tracks to be bent by trains, and tried to hitch rides on freight cars just as they began to move. We were always daring each other to do that. It would not have been a crime, of course. But it would have taken us over that edge of irreversible violence where, whether in a pattern of years or in the flicker of an oversight, crime begins.

"Far from it. Far from it," he is muttering to himself again.

Every child, naturally, who was not a sissy swam. In lakes, and seas, and heavily chlorinated pools, they earned their certificates, Beginners, Intermediate, Advanced, Junior Life Saving, Senior Life Saving—all the New England summer accreditations of the healthy child. There has been, always, the preoccupation of people of our age and class with documents: degrees, cards, certifications, records, licenses. One got them the year one became of age to get them. Of age. People who missed their proper year often remained afraid of swimming, driving, hunting, or whatever, all their lives. The accreditations all began, though, in the water: at five, the dog paddle, and at twelve, the dive to break the death grip of some giant instructor, in order to tow him, by means of the chin carry, the hair carry, the cross-chest carry, whatever other carry, home. By now, there have been many years of accepted assurances that the water's fine—quite warm, actually—once you get into it; many years' insane passings on of such an assurance. And here we all are. All that is, except Barney, whose sailboat overturned two years ago last November. It is probable that he had been drinking. When Jim and I took him to dinner the preceding August, he said he was bored with his job.

"Now, class. Now, seniors," the high school principal said, interrupting the pledge. "It's one nation. Under Gawd. Indivisible. Some of you are saying under Gahd. In fact, most of you. What are the parents going to think? What are your teachers going to think? What are the visitors from Hartford going to think? This is very important. Many of you are college bound. Now say with me, please. Gawd. Again. Gawd. *Un*der Gawd. *In*divisible. Good. Now let's resume. Give it the feeling you're going to give it on graduation day." Her name was Miss Crosby. Crawsby, not Crahsby. We let it pass.

From her earliest childhood, Jametta Anna Scozzafava had mysterious sources of information about what holiday it was. No school tomorrow, she would say—often quite late for a small child to be up on a cold evening: Scragg Day, or Teachers' Records Day, Moss Day, State Commemoration Day, or High School Bus Repairs. Mysteriously, these holidays did exist, although few of them recurred from year to year. Jametta also knew holiday nights: Chalk Night, Garbage Night, Crab Night—and, I think, Teachers' Records Night, although I am not sure. Chalk Night and Garbage Night were clear enough. I never knew what were the right observances for Crab Night and, one year, for Seven Moon. From third grade on, Jametta spent most of her classroom hours either whispering with Moose Natale, or absent altogether with the Passcard. In her senior year, however, Jametta sat in front of one Alvin Benso, in the first row of Miss Keane's English class. We were doing our required Shakespeare play. The state seemed to require of its students one half year of world history, Mesopotamia to the present; one half year of American history, Jamestown to the present; one solid year of Biology, in which one earthworm and one frog must be dissected; and, somewhere in four years of English classes, a Shakespeare play. Miss Keane's method of teaching Shakespeare was to assign parts for reading by row, characters in order of appearance: first seat, first row, first part, and so on along the rows. The class was doing *The Merchant of Venice,* Miss Keane's favorite. Miss Keane had done her disquisition about Shylock—a villain she found comparable, and perhaps even related, to all the many traitors in our own time, our own country, brainwashing our boys abroad, flashing subliminal messages on television, stealthily approaching, if they did not already have, our minds. Miss Keane had subsided. The reading started. Jametta was Portia. It fell to Alvin to read Lorenzo. "Lorenzo Benso!" Jametta shouted. "Lorenzo Benso!" swept the classroom. It was our first political slogan, and the witticism of Jametta's academic life.

"Far from it," the shuffling man is muttering to himself again. "Far from it."

The Albany legislator wept as he cast his vote. His brother-in-law was up for a judgeship. He had no choice. "I will hear no ill spoken of Rosa Addio," the head of a local school board said. "She is a fine Christian woman." The lobbyist for the teachers union blanched. "Now, on the Alabama resolution," the convention speaker said to the delegates in caucus, "you can vote your conscience. Or with your union." "Ah, jobs, jobs in the ghetto," said the tenured pedant on the investigating committee that, yearly, covers up corruption in our branch of the city university. "Ghetto jobs is our *bête noire*. Excuse me."

The clerk of the morgue of this paper is an irascible man. Reporters are always taking his files away, forgetting to sign for them, keeping them, losing them, throwing them away. Over the years, it has made the clerk ill. I signed for a file, took the folder to my desk, and then took it home. Everybody does it. It is against the rules. After four days, I brought the folder back. The clerk of the morgue was incensed. What, he demanded to know, if the man whose file it was had died in those four days; what, in the absence of the file, would the obituary have been constructed from —had I considered that at all? Well, I said, since I had signed for the file, if the man whose file it was had died, somebody could have called me up. I would have brought the folder back. True, the clerk said, but there were questions of another sort. What if, in those four days, a new fact about the man had come to light, a fact that ought quite surely to be added to the file; what, in the absence of the file, was there to add the fact to, what rubric, category, or place was there to put the new fact in—had I considered that at all, had I given it one moment's thought? I said I had not. The clerk, becoming pale with rage, said he might

151

have to raise the matter with management. People seem to be unhappy in so many different ways. I've always liked the wrathful keepers of the files.

"What you say is true," the professor said, staring through his study window at the sky, "but not so very interesting."

He ran up the stairs and they were after him. He fumbled with his keys, opened the door, slammed it behind him and listened for their breathing and for their steps. He heard their steps first, heavy feet on the carpeted stairs; then, he heard breathing. He looked through the peep-hole in his door and saw, as usual, nothing. He turned suddenly, caught his own reflection abruptly in the mirror, and nearly scared himself to death.

"I have a collect call for anyone from . . ."
"Yes, operator. That's fine."
"Miss Fain in Wash . . ."
"That's fine, operator. I accept the . . ."
" . . . ington, D.C. Will you accept the charges?"
"Thank you. Yes."

Sometimes cooperation impedes the gist. Someone, many people probably, had urinated in the phone booth. That is common. Many things serve something other than their original, unarguable purpose. The left lane, for example, on the highway. Some people use it because they prefer it. Some people use it because it looks like any other. Some people use it for some other reason. But the thing is, you are supposed to be driving faster if you use that lane.

"Hello, Jim?"
"Hi."
"Just a moment, please. I have a collect call for anyone from . . ."
"Yes, operator. That's fine. *I accept the charges.*"

"Hello, Jim. I'm . . ."

"Go ahead, please. Your party is on the line."

The slowest-talking man I know tends to loom in elevator doors, in hallways, booths, and other narrow places. He coughs, nods to himself, begins a sentence, continues nodding to himself in all the pauses along what he has to say. Eating with him is a problem. He chews so thoroughly. He raises his fork, speaks, pauses in midsentence, nods, takes what is on his fork, meditates, chews. When he swallows, one thinks he is about to say his sentence to the end. But no, he loads his fork again, eats, nods in silence, has a little sip of coffee and another mouthful before going on. One tends to drink a lot on these occasions. Agreement stalls him. Sometimes, when it has been clear for several phrases just what Moe is going to say, when one has been standing, for example, in the rain beside a taxi one had hailed at the very instant Moe loomed, one tries to complete his sentence for him. It slows him down. He waves his hand irritably, as though warding off a swarm of gnats, before his face. He moves his head like a pitcher shaking off a signal that he does not like. Then he starts again, nodding, waving, pausing, finishing his sentence in his own good time.

"Hello, Jim. I guess they've fired me."

"They have?"

"Yeah."

"Well, it just isn't our day, then. I've just been chased all the way up the stairs from the hallway, by what looked like two crazies."

"You ought to call the police."

"No. They're gone. I heard the outside door shut."

"Well, then. How are you?"

"O.K. And you?"

"Fine, I guess. Unemployed."

"Oh, well. You can always . . ."

"The number you have dialed is not in service at this time.

Please place your call again or dial your . . ."

" . . . teach or something."

"I guess so. This isn't . . ."

" . . . operator, and she will be able to help you."

" . . . much of a connection."

"No."

"The number you have dialed . . ."

"Hello, hello. Ida. Will you drop it?"

"And my client feels that unless there has been substantial compliance by . . ."

" . . . Rotunda. Thank you, Ron. WCBS Newstime is four . . ."

" . . . and Muriel. Overnight. Enough. Never, frankly, have I . . ."

"Jim, I think we better . . ."

"Is this Washington 225-8462?"

"No, it isn't."

"Could I speak with Ramón."

" . . . but the highest respect for him close quote, paragraph."

"Iss no here."

"Would you read me that again, please? Beginning . . ."

"Allo, allo. Ramón?"

"Iss no here."

"Jim, I'll try . . ."

" . . . and costly litigation. Moreover, there is nothing . . ."

" . . . on hold for twenty-two minutes. I don't call that stepped out. I call that . . ."

" . . . or anybody else. I won't drop it. Let him drop it. If they . . ."

" . . . freezes over close quote, paragraph. Do you get the . . ."

" . . . such rudeness. Well, she hung up. But I made the . . ."

" . . . in the second sentence?"

"No, I don't."

"Ramón? Ramón? Allo . . ."

"Iss no here."

" . . . simple question. Is it dead, or isn't it? I have been . . ."

"Jim, this connection is really . . ."

"Mark you, Mr. Ambogewe. We will not subscribe to any such . . ."

" . . . awful."

"Yeah."

The restaurant on Jim's corner has three pillars, one at the back, one near the entrance, one in the middle of the wall behind the bar. On the pillar nearest the entrance, there is a dart board. You have to pass behind that pillar to enter or to leave the restaurant, to use the phone, to hang and to pick up your coat. In front of the pillar, people throw their darts. The pillar, it is true, is broad. The dart board has now been on it for six months. Nobody seems to mind or mention it. I try not to look in that direction when we're there. The owner of the restaurant, who used to be an editor on night rewrite, is an extremely literal-minded man. He would be reluctant, for example, to infer from rabbit tracks in a forest that, not just four rabbit's feet, connected in a manner yet to be established, but, in all probability, an entire living rabbit has passed by. This made working with him, when he was still at the paper, a little slow. It also means that he will not move that dart board until he has hard evidence that is what he ought to do.

"Don't dwell on it," the shuffling man is now saying to himself. "Don't dwell on it."

Jim works for the candidate just about full time now. I'm surprised that I hate it, but I do. For a time, our people used to mill about, saying "The system works. The system works" —the way kids used to run off the field shouting "We won. We won. We won," when the game had been called on account of rain, or darkness, or because somebody had decided to take his baseball home. I am sure it does work, or I hope it does, and I used to think it did; but I was glad when we could all stop saying that.

I am the Paul Revere of the morning phone call. There are social ladies one may call at 8:45 A.M.; their lines are busy. Two minutes earlier, one wakes them up. Most people at the paper sleep till eleven or noon. Jim has breakfast at six. When I used to go to Washington, I took the first morning shuttle. In phone calls, I am somehow always, always on the early side.

"My daughter, you see," said the drunk man, who had not yet quite mastered the idiom, "is a Jesus creep."

"Freak," said the girl on his right.

"I beg your pardon?"

"Jesus freak," the girl said, politely.

"Yes. That's what they call it. So I said to my wife, Look here. Saint *John* was a Jesus creep. Saint *Paul* was a Jesus creep. Saint *Fran*cis was a Jesus creep." (He sent these italics bravely leaning off into the wind.) "Why, everyone doing God's *work* is a Jesus creep. It's a new way of saying Christian, that's what it is. Mother said, Be that as it may. I don't care for it."

There is a flower shop in the arcade under the Pentagon. A whole floor of the Pentagon is filled with stores, clothing and camera shops, bookstores, boutiques. In the days when our staff resignations began, I sent Phil Eisen, our boss, and his girl African violets from that flower shop, after a dinner at their house. Since it would be awkward to call and ask, Did you or did you not receive those Pentagon African violets, I guess I'll never know whether they received them or not. Then Phil resigned. I had a drink with him the night he left. When I first met him in Washington, Phil was the fattest man I'd ever seen. That night, he was extremely thin. I couldn't think of anything to say. I said, "Phil, you've lost weight." He said he had gained ninety pounds in fifty days, he had been so very angry in his work. Then, he had become angrier still, and lost a hundred thirty-two. The change had come when he began to write a book. Every piece of news, any turn of events at all, had this quality: it depressed him utterly. I asked whether his book was done. He said it was. I asked how long it was. "Eight hundred and ninety-seven pages," he said. Then he added, earnestly, "You don't suppose they'll think I wrote it in a fit of pique."

"It's not so bad," the professor said. "It only isn't wonderful. Nobody has an obligation to be wonderful."

My argument with the psychiatrist of Jim's younger brother, Simon, was as follows: whether the natural gait of the horse is, in fact, the gallop or the trot. I said it was the trot. He said it was the gallop. Or the other way around. The point is that we insisted, all through dinner; we pursued it for a long, long time. It is not an argument that ramifies much. Within the first few seconds one has said about all there is to say. There are many such questions, which, once they are stated, are completed. Does Macy's tell Gimbel's, for example, does not ramify. You have got no further if you go on to Does Saks tell Bendel's, does Bonwit's tell Bergdorf's, does Chanel tell Givenchy, does Woolworth tell Kresge's, does Penn Station tell Grand Central, does Best's tell Peck and Peck? You are no longer expounding a proposition. You are having a tantrum. Simon's psychiatrist and I pursued our tantrum, in duet, all evening long. The horse might have two natural gaits, the Charleston and the entrechat, for all it mattered. I meant, I didn't like the man and I thought that, within twenty years, his profession would have vanished, leaving no artifacts of any interest except a dazed memory of fifty years of ineffective and remunerative peculation in the work of a single artist, Freud. I also meant I didn't like his flowered shirt. He meant, I think, he didn't like me, either.

"Sarah now is twenty-one, twenty-one, twenty-one," we used to sing in the dining room. "Sarah now is twenty-one.

And safe from King Farouk." On days when it was nobody's birthday, we sang something that went "My father killed a kangaroo. Gave me the gristly part to chew. Wasn't that a terrible thing to do. He gave me to chew the gristly part of the kangaroo." It was not clear why this particular lament should be sung so often in a distinguished academic institution. Perhaps it was for relief from the plainsong, the madrigals, the lovely, authentic, but somehow wildly misplaced old ballads we were always singing, in the cloisters, in the dining rooms, at the foot of the bell tower, wherever some tradition or other required that these songs be sung.

"All acts are acts of aggression, we know that," the professor said. "The point is to give them other properties."

The wallflower sat reading in the Paris restaurant. There used to be so many categories of wallflower: the anxious, smiling, tense ones who leaned forward, trying; the important, busy, apparently elsewhere preoccupied ones, who were nonetheless waiting, waiting in the carpeted offices of their inattention, to be found. There were wallflowers who clustered noisily together, and others who worked a territory, resolute and alone. And then, there were wallflowers who had recognized for years that the thing was hopeless, who had found in that information a kind of calm. They no longer tried, with a bright and desperate effort, to sustain a conversation with somebody's brother, somebody's usher, somebody's roommate, somebody's roommate's usher's brother, or, worst of all, with that male wallflower who ought—by God who ought—to be an ally, who could, in dignity and the common interest, join forces to make it through an evening, but who, after all, had higher aspirations, and neither the sense nor the courtesy to conceal it, who, in short, scorned the partner fate and the *placement* had dealt him, worst of all. The category of wallflower who had given up on all this was very quiet, not indifferent, only quiet. And she always brought a book.

The wallflower, then, was reading in her neighborhood Paris restaurant. The regular customers sat at their accustomed tables. It was nine-thirty on a busy night. She had finished her meal and ordered coffee. The light in the restaurant was pleasant. She read on. A tall, blond, shaggy man had been coming to the restaurant almost every evening of the autumn. He always sat at a small table near hers and ordered a single cup of coffee. He sat, with that single cup of coffee, most nights from nine until the restaurant closed. He was there, as usual, this evening. Her coffee did not come. She read. Her awareness of the shaggy man was, as it was of the restaurant in general, peripheral. In addition to his coffee, he had ordered brandy. He seemed altogether somehow less poor. Suddenly, though quietly, he offered her a cigarette. She upset her wineglass. *"Ça vous scandalise?"* he said.

"She feels she doesn't want to anchor the hat."
"I'm not talking about now. Now is different."
"Whatever it is they want from him is not what is there."

The freshmen, who had been at the top of their classes through high school, got C's on their first college midterms, and felt the world tilt. Within months, they had caught on to serious study, had learned to set forth information, with that last, original fillip of the expert mind. In default of the fillip, when invention failed them, they used the fail-safe method for undergraduate work at any solid institution: take two utterly unrelated things or matters and show that they are, if not in fact identical, actually related in the most profound and subtle sense. A paper of this sort would demonstrate, not only the highest tradition of the scholar, but also the signature of the alert undergraduate, her mark. For lectures, the intense, off-the-beat academic flirtation: the animated face, the gaze at the instructor, the lowered eyes when that look was returned; the secret smile at anything that could remotely be construed as felicitous or comic; the hastily scribbled work in notebooks, not when points were being made in order or by number, but at some demonstrably arbitrary moment, when the instructor had not realized that his lecture had reached such a highly interesting point. The crude strategies of the years preceding college, the raised hand, the eager question, were despised, and rightly. "Tell Thorne to shut up," on a scrap with a fragment of a doodle, was passed, in complete consensus, all the way across the room to Bronx Science graduate Thorne. Having refined her display of rapt attention to changes rung on silence, Thorne went on to marry a tycoon and run a clinic for unmanageably disturbed children. The style of flirtation specific to classrooms was of service to the students all their lives.

"So for these purposes, digitalis, adamantine, apple orchard, gonorrhea, labyrinthine, motherfucker, flights of fancy, Duffy's Tavern, Halley's Comet, birthday present, xenophobic are all synonyms," the great professor said. "Synonyms, in terms of meter, that is."

"I see."

"And words that rhyme," he said, "are synonyms, in terms of rhyme, with all the words they rhyme with. Cat, gnat, flat. Fang, sang, sprang, you see."

"Yes."

"So that in the study of poetics, we have. Rhyme synonyms. And meter synonyms. I leave aside pure synonyms of meaning. There are not really very many. And there are other factors, of course."

"Of course."

"In tests of free word association, we find that some people respond in ways that reflect what we might call the cast of mind of synonyms. You might say trap. They say snare. You say dog. They say cat. More or less equivalences, don't you see.

"Other people have what we call the turn of mind of context. You say trap. They say door. You say cat. They say

160

hairs. Contextual associations. Can you give me another rhyme synonym for flat, Miss Miller?"

"Sprat."

"Yes. And another meter synonym for apple orchard, Mr. Elkin?"

"Vigilante."

"And a free word association, in the line of synonyms, to church, Miss Wheelock?"

"Temple."

"And a context response to church, Mr. Cook?"

"Apse."

"Exactly. Fine. You will see at once that every choice in language is determined, on every plane, rhyme, meter, meaning, other planes, by a factor of synonymy. And one of contexture. If you do not see it, I refer you to your Jakobson and Halle.

"At first, we thought the distinction of no practical importance. Then, we found that, in cases of severe speech disorder, the absolute extremes turn out, in fact, to be, at one end, cases of pure synonymy, and at the other, pure cases of context. In disorders of synonymy, the same word is repeated, endlessly. Repetition. At the extreme of context, we have words rambling, with no apparent coherence. What we have come to call a word heap."

"A word heap."

"Yes.

"Now, if we turn from poetics to other fields—anthropology for instance—we find surprising applications. I draw your attention to the Haida, a tribe of Indians in the Northwest. The normal process of elimination seemed to them a sad thing; when they encountered droppings or dung in the fields or forests, they said a little prayer of condolence to the animal they thought it lost to. The first brave of the tribe, in the first times, was courting one of two sisters. The other sister was jealous and forlorn. On the path to the sisters' home, this brave one day noticed a pile of excrement which,

161

in the course of his many journeys, had grown nearly to his own size. He asked it, as it were, to pull itself together and marry the other sister. It did so. From the marriages of the two sisters, the tribe descends."

"Really."

"Now, what we have here might be considered a disorder of synonym in the name of context. Marriage, usually, is a matter of synonymy, equation. Husband, wife. Boy, girl. In some cases, brother, sister. But here we have a marriage of a person with an object with which that person is, as it were, only contextually associated. There are other considerations, of course. But wherever we look—poetics, psychology, anthropology, linguistics—the two ideas, synonymy and contexture, are among the key structures and processes of the mind."

On the other hand, our local controversy is whether we ought to require the ability to read at an eighth-grade level before we let any university student in. I can't understand how that is the question. Surely we are obligated to give them, at least, an eighth-grade education while they're here and before we send them out. "I found the whole work disappointing," Nina Valindez, a student in one of my own courses, here in the city, wrote, in her paper last term. "It was more theatrical than filmic. It did, however, remind me of many nineteenth-century novels such as *Vanity Fair* by Thakkry. And many of the better novels of Jane Austen." Pat Gertz, one of my best students, wrote a paper on "The Sorted Love Affair in Fiction of the Forties." The paper expressed all the views that a student of my generation might have held, of which affairs were and which were not to be considered "sorted." And yet. And Shelley Muess. Ms. Muess, who had received a passing grade, left many agitated messages last term, after midnight, on my answering service. She warned that she would have to take our case to the Student Faculty Grievance Committee and enter a Denunciation/Demerit against my record with the Faculty Appraisal Board. I called her back. I asked what the trouble was. She said she had never received less than honors grades before. Since it had been a matter of some importance to me that I not actually flunk anybody in this intellectual swamp and rip-off I mentioned that the exam had only required each student to list the films shown in the course. Students were allowed to help one another with it, to take it home and turn it in the following week. Since Shelley Muess had missed most of the films, and misspelled the ones she got, a passing grade seemed to me not ungenerous. "Well," Shelley said, hardly able to breathe with indignation, "I'm not an English major." The chancellor of our branch of the university once asked me what I thought of the head of our division now. I said I thought he was a thug. "Ah," she said, with a chiming laugh and a lilt, clapping her hands just once. "You *writers!* What a way you have with words." For the most part, the students treat me with grave, gentle concern, as though I were something strange—a giraffe, say—among them, or an apprentice on a tightrope, or one of their own on a bad trip.

They were saying "Make peace, not war," and so, the Commander of the Ohio State National Guard testified in the course of the Kent State trials, he threw a rock at them.

Dinner was over. Almost everybody had gone home. Jim and I were clearing the table. Benjamin, a tousled young journalist who was covering the negotiations at City Hall, was happily drinking up what remained in everybody's butter dish. He did this without comment, as though it were the ordinary thing to do after a dinner that included melted butter. When he had finished, he drank what remained in three cups of coffee, and sat down on the sofa, with a perfect grin.

The girls were always running out of money, out of cash, precisely, to pay taxi drivers, train conductors, men who delivered pizzas after dark. They borrowed cash, normally, upon arrival. They borrowed passions—Wallace Stevens, Joseph Conrad, Mozart, hiking, the Bible—from each other, as girls of another generation borrowed clothes. At the great universities in those years, everyone who was not doing philosophy, in the mode that liked to think of itself as Ordinary Language, was in one of the other jargons, usually the social sciences. The philosophers at the great universities were, without exception, failed mathematicians. When they were not examining much of the vocabulary of civilized discourse to conclude that it, after all, lacked meaning, they muttered Gödel, Russell, Hilbert, liking to imply that they themselves had chosen philosophy over mathematics to give themselves a wider, though related intellectual field. With an intoxication they derived otherwise only from drinking a little sherry or from being in the presence of somebody English, they required and flunked their undergraduates, year after year, in a course called Symbolic Logic, much as the social scientists, who didn't understand mathematics either, liked to flunk their students in a course called Statistics 101. Many students had been frightened by even the mention of algebra or numbers, ever since their first struggles with long division, and ever since someone first told them, most often wrongly as it turned out, that their skills were verbal skills. The predicament of these students enabled professors in all the departments that were a disgrace to the humanities in those years to claim for their work a strong mathematical base. The serious colleges for women were, by contrast, solid. They taught the same courses, without fuss and with a small sigh; they taught other foolish courses, notably in education, that way too. They reserved their serious efforts for the medievalists, the true scientists, linguists, other scholars, even the pre-law and pre-medical students, all of whom went out, degree in hand, into the world, and were asked, like their predecessors, whether they could type.

"Can you have dinner Thursday night?" Simon asked. Jim was in Atlanta. "It will be very late. Have a sandwich or something before. I'll pick you up at seven. Don't ask where we're going. It will be a surprise." The surprise was a five-hour performance of *Parsifal*. This implied a misunderstanding so profound that I kept looking at Simon from time to time to see whether he meant it as a shaggy-dog sort of joke. Mostly, he was asleep. Whenever he woke up, he was so evidently happy to be there, at that interminable spectacle in that vast auditorium with too few aisles. He would grin. I would grin. He would go back to sleep. The worst part, I think, comes near the end, when the hermit sings to Parsifal about how wonderful it is that Parsifal has brought the Spear, which will, after so many years, relieve the suffering of Amfortas, the Fisher King. The aria itself lasts many years. One is aware of Amfortas, waiting in pain, while this long-winded hermit and Parsifal exchange congratulations and amenities. Narrative conventions do make it quite impossible for them to bring the king the Spear, and *then,* when he is no longer in pain, sing on about their sympathy for him, in all those years, and their great gladness that a remedy is at hand. The whole magic of a plot requires that somebody be impeded from getting something over with. Yet there one is, with an emotional body English almost, wishing that pole-vaulter over his bar, wanting something to happen or not to happen, wishing somebody well. Amfortas was not even on stage. In fact, there was no Amfortas. Yet, more than I wished that I were elsewhere, more than I wished that the opera were over, I did wish that they would bring that king his Spear. When it was over, Simon, who is really a musician, woke up, cheered, applauded. He is also chief resident in surgery at a city hospital. When he isn't on call, he studies voice. "Wasn't it wonderful," he said.

The athletes among us were extremely delicate, subject to injuries and colds. Avalanches fell on them. Their stomachs were easily upset. When Ralph's girl left him for a year in Paris, he, after two beers, leaped over a cliff and missed whatever he muzzily thought of as his destination, and hit a tree, and broke his jaw in sixteen places. His girl returned to him. His jaw was wired. He got the flu. When we were younger, we all thought we liked to swim. Tired, shivering, we pleaded to stay in. Now, at the fifth stroke of what begins as a brazen crawl, my feet sink. I have to swim some other stroke. Once, Alice, a true and natural athlete, jumped into the pool of a hotel outside Palermo and swam her crawl. She had already played an hour of tennis, and ridden one of the furry island horses. She felt that her exercise for the day was not complete. So she swam. At her third lap of the long pool, an Italian, who had been lying in the sun, simply could no longer stand it. He dived in, began the crawl. They did two laps, Alice in the lead. At her fifth lap, he was already half a pool behind her. He speeded up. His feet were lagging. At her nineteenth lap, he gave it up. He was enraged. In her energy, her good nature, her athleticism, Alice sometimes forgets that we are not all alike. Just recently, she took Idris to the kitchen to show him what she called a beautiful surprise. Idris is the most cultivated, gentle, pacific man we know; he also is a vegetarian. Alice opened the refrigerator door and there, looking alert and almost confiding, was, from her last hunt, the head of a decapitated fox.

The child of nature, with a sunburned stomach and dirt on its wrists, had followed the wrong fur sleeve at the supermarket. He was now quite lost. He began to sob, wetly, hysterically—not like a scared, lost child but in the manner of a tyrannical, mean, accusatory brat. "You're not my mother," he began to shout, a natural informer, at the pale, wrong lady in the near fur coat, and then, "She's not my mother," when he had gathered a sympathetic little crowd. "Lady, are you this kid's mother?" the supermarket manager asked the lady. She said she wasn't. He said, "Well, then why don't you leave him alone?" When Sally, one of our legal reporters, went to the hospital for a hysterectomy, we visited her by turns. Carl was there on the second afternoon. When the nurse asked him to leave the room for a moment, he naturally left. "Now,

Mother, here we are," the nurse said. She brought some-body's baby in. Sally, who does have two children, was con-fused. She said, "Wait, just a minute." The nurse cooed. Sally pointed out that the baby wasn't hers. "Now, Mother," the nurse said, "in large hospitals we often think that. But baby knows. Baby has a wristlet." Then she looked at the wristlet, said "Oh, now," one last time, and, holding the baby, walked out.

"Harry," the blonde said, waving her drink and putting out her cigarette, "do you realize you have made yourself into a person that one has to lie to?"

"Janine," he said, "you know I'm very tired of your *aper-çus?*"

What was mortifying was the limbo dancing. What was mortifying was the fat, hot, drunk, sunburned and flattered man at whom the calypso lyrics were directed. What was mortifying was the way his wife danced with the famous, tense, witless insult comedian. What was mortifying was the insinuating child who recited "Horatio at the Bridge" in its entirety. "Sweetie," the blonde screamed from the dance floor to her adolescent grandson, "isn't this fun?"

I never liked him, and now he is dead. Perhaps I should wish that I had liked him better. But I do not wish it. And I did not like him. I was not asked, which is just as well. What he was, was asleep. So they should not have buried him. Hindsight is easy. Mistakes will happen. It was one of a series of errors that marked his whole life. Not the last error, it now seems. His will is under litigation. The penulti-mate error, perhaps.

It was his misfortune to die during the strike of the Ceme-tery Workers and Greens Attendants Union—oddly enough, in this city, Local 365. I covered the meeting at which the strike ended. The men had not tended a grave or buried a body in months. The head of the local, in describing his problems, with the diocese, the bereaved, the bureaus of public health and sanitation, spoke eloquently of "this tragic backlog" and "this extra grief." At Mount Carmel, Calvary, Cyprus Hills, there had been vandalism. The unburied coolly bided their time. The trouble is he was our candidate, Jim's candidate really. It can't be helped. That is all.

Our anachronism. The young uptown doctor found his standard of living drastically threatened by the change in the law. He had worked hard through his schooling, internship, and residency. He had married a girl he had met at a mixer, at Goucher. They had settled in Rye. Every Thursday night, beginning at midnight and ending at eight in the morning, he had been performing abortions, for years. The rates he had charged had not been steep, when compared with the cost of a trip to some other country. Occasionally, for a young actress out of work or some other demonstrably poor patient, he had done the operation for free. On some Thursday nights, there were only two patients. Sometimes, in the fall, there were seven. His preferred number for any Thursday night was four. He called all his patients—the Thursday night ones and those in his regular practice—by their first names. He insisted that they call him Ned. When abortion in New York became legal, Ned, never having thought of the problem in these terms, faced the prospect of having his income reduced by two thousand dollars a week, cash.

He had never been a man without scruples. The legal risk he had taken, through the years, for his patients, a sense that sane, prosperous men did not pay taxes on cash income, and a vague liberal perception that it was not altogether right to support an already too powerful government—these had combined in Ned's thoughts into a moral certainty that his Thursday-night income was not subject to the income tax. He had, anyway, of late been taking losses in the market. Sheila, his wife, was in analysis. His two daughters were in therapy. His son—he did not know what to think about his son. At five, the boy already lacked stamina, lacked ambition. He seemed a happy little boy, but there was no question that he was far behind Doug and Netta Forster's five-year-old in intellectual development and motor control. He was also far less tall. Doug was Ned's best friend, and Ned had hated him since their earliest childhood. Doug had been something of an athlete. Doug had won full scholarships for college and medical school. It was true that Ned had not required scholarships, but the fact was that he had not had them. In the Army, Doug had met somebody with whom he had invested in real estate in Arizona. Ever since, it seemed clear that he was marginally richer than Ned had ever been. To conceal this fact, this disparity, had so far been the most expensive proposition of Ned and Sheila's lives.

When the law changed, Ned had to consider these and other enormous pressures. He decided to make no concession whatever to that change. He needed the money. He had ten years of Thursday-night patients as evidence that, when they needed him, he was a good and kindly man. Patients trusted him, just as they always had, just as they should have. When a girl or a woman now came to him, not wanting to be pregnant and believing that she was, he told her to come to his office Thursday night. In a very short time, he found himself instructing patients to do this, whether the tests showed they were actually pregnant or not. He justified this to himself in a number of ways. He was busy. They were anxious. For patients beyond their early twenties, the operation might be advisable anyway. Or he could use the occasion to install an intrauterine device.

The result of this rationalization was that, on Thursday nights, Ned's waiting room was a perfect anachronism. The women, girls usually, who arrived there were nervous, embarrassed. They did not want to be seen by the others. At the same time, each thought that the others looked legitimate. Perhaps they really *were* there for that intrauterine device. The receptionist had a bright and unwavering poster smile. She sat there, with country-and-western music blaring from her transistor, checking people in. By eleven-fifteen, when the last patient had usually come in, the receptionist left.

On any given Thursday, there might be a fifteen-year-old, shy, not pretty, accompanied by an overbearing, overcheerful mother; another young woman, perhaps a grade-school teacher, evidently religious, miserable, praying, removing her rosary from a purse and then replacing it, uncertain whether she could use a rosary on such a day or not. One young, engaged couple. One apparently adulterous young wife, alone. But whereas what had brought people to Ned's office before the law changed was usually something savvy, something knowledgeable in having gotten such an address at all, what the people in Ned's office now had in common was ignorance, and perhaps shame. Just as he put each one of them to sleep, with his own special intravenous formula, he said, "Just you wait. You'll find this a kind of high." Then he worked on his patients, one by one, through the night. None of them had complications. None of them died. The jet, the Xerox, the abortion law, and of course, of course, the tape recorder—these advances in terms of the reversible and the irreversible are one line, one still fuzzy line, between our set and the last set and the next.

There are only so many plots. There are insights, prose flights, rhythms, felicities. But only so many plots. At a slower pace, in a statelier world, the equations are statelier. The mayor has run off with the alderman's wife, and it was to be expected if one looks back. The mayor and the alderman won't confide in each other or be doubles partners any more. The other consequences, it will turn out, might have been foreseen. In three households and two generations, and the treehouse instantly, the track, to a degree, can still be kept. But here, the inevitable is being interrupted by strangers all the time. Seven people go off into the sunset, and the eighth is the custodian of the plot. There were so few variations. I had begun to believe that a story line was a conceit like any other. One has only to take to bed, though, with a Seconal and a thriller, racing toward their confrontation, for it to become clear that this is not quite the case. The plot of

170

things converging, as in *Appointment in Samarra,* as in love stories, as in any story where a rendezvous must be kept. The plot of things separating, not so common, disintegration, breaking up. The plot of one thing following in the track of another, as in thrillers, chases. The plot of things parallel. Suspense, which has time as an obstacle to a resolution in the future. Nostalgia, which has time as an obstacle to a resolution in the past. Maybe there are stories, even, like solitaire or canasta; they are shuffled and dealt, then they do or they do not come out. Or the deck falls on the floor. Or a piece of country music, a quartet, a parade, the flag—all the things one ought by now to be too old for—touch, whatever it is.

A few years ago, the wire services reported that, on account of a defective latch, the cargo door on a DC-10 opened, in flight. A coffin fell out. A lady at work in her flower garden saw what she took to be a coffin fall from the sky into a neighboring field. Having been recently widowed, the lady made the obvious inference. She put down her trowel, drove to the nearest state asylum, and committed herself. When reporters reached her, to tell her the thing had really happened, and to ask her reaction to it, the lady said she preferred to stay right where she was. There has been no further news of her, or of the lady in the supermarket. Twenty years later, however, the kid accuser in the supermarket may be gaining seniority as a congressman.

The Begum played Scrabble. Morning, afternoon, and night, on the beach, aboard the boat, in the harbor night club, with ordinary sets, or Scrabble dice, or cleated letters for use on jolting surfaces, the Begum played. The Russians had smuggled in a cheese, of which they were proud. Nobody else cared much for it. Apparently, as in the matter of wines, there exists an international body of experts, which rates cheese. Last year, for the first time, the Soviet Union invited this committee to come and test its cheeses. The committee had pronounced itself unable to distinguish between any single Russian cheese and any other—except one, which, on the basis of its smell and general appearance, the committee members unanimously declined even to taste. The Russians on our island always passed around this cheese.

We sat on the beach. The Queen was an inexhaustible swimmer. Somebody had to be with her at all times to see that she did not feel lonely or drown. She talked while she swam. Ralph, who could make conversation while swimming, was with her. He was subject to chills; when he came out of the water after one of these long swims, he would stammer with cold. His girl and her brother were sitting beside us. Being naturally fair, they were now very sunburned. They stayed wrapped in their towels, and did crosswords, or tuned in to their program of news from the mainland, or did whatever else seemed amiable, or kind, or polite.

When Jim's friends from the days when he was in the O.S.S. first settled there, they tried to raise cattle, for milk. There were already small herds of wild cattle, from past generations, at large in the hills. Within a few weeks, the wild cows, having entered the pastures by night, had lured the tame cattle into the hills with them. Now wild cows and tame cows, side by side, would come thundering through the palms of an evening, churning up the few flower beds and grazing on the few lawns there were. People began to surround their lawns with enormous rolls of barbed wire. Every carefully watered green thing was now fortified against the cows.

At City Hall, as on the campus, negotiations are in progress. It is not at all clear to me what a negotiation is. Union and management, say, terrorist and foreign minister, buyer and seller, kidnapper and F.B.I. agent, husband and wife, at least two parties anyway, disagree. They exchange views. A strike, perhaps, a war, a bankruptcy, a murder, a divorce impends. One side begins, and claims it can accept no less. The other responds, saying it can afford no more. It is clear to both sides, from the start, that both positions are false.

They proceed to bargain then, in what is called good faith. Bad faith exists when a side takes both positions to be absolutely true, then deals with something other than negotiation in its heart—stalling for time, for instance, so that friends can arrive and bomb the house. Good faith negotiation requires a liar's margin of some sort. "I can't stand it," somebody says. "I can't help it," someone else replies. Justice is called upon, as well. At City Hall, when they negotiate, the parties get a little sleep on the floors of rooms across a hall. Night after night. In Teheran, in the oil negotiations of 1971, a representative of the companies absent-mindedly left a memo on the bargaining table during the lunch break of the first day. The memo outlined the companies' fallback position on any compromise that they could consider tolerable. A reporter bought the memo from a janitor. It was published in the paper the next morning. The fallback position became the position at which the talks began; the remainder of the negotiation entailed the companies' retreat from their original last stand. The absent-mindedness, almost everyone agreed, was real.

In the matter of jobs, I think I know nine spies. Eight are American. One is foreign. One has dual citizenship. It is hard to know what they do, exactly, except that they are inexhaustibly gregarious. It is not thinkable that any of the nine could learn, or for that matter keep, a secret. I am certain that they do not hover over microfilms or denounce friends. Two date starlets. One lives from time to time with debutantes, now divorced, whom he has known since boarding school. I guess what these spies—if they are spies, and I'm sure they are—are paid to do is observe trends. Why any government should pay them to observe trends is not clear to me. It may be that there are times when any information about anything whatever seems to have a reassuring, valid quality. More likely, spying is one more featherbedding, overpaid bureaucracy. Certainly all nine are snobs, with manifold, even catholic, snobberies: class, money, power, fame, fad, culture, byline, notoriety. They are all best men at controversial second weddings; escorts of abandoned wives; godfathers of very late litters of children; fixtures at black-tie dinners for convicted forgers who have published memoirs and for rehabilitated dope pushers and stranglers who hold visiting professorships of Urban Planning and Reform.

Each of the nine seems to be liked by everyone except the other eight. Our agents are fluent in at least a second language, but then we all are. I don't know why we were not all asked to be agents, but we weren't. The only one who claims he was and who now drinks and talks a lot about it is Lane Prell, who needs to be an authority on most matters. Whenever the C.I.A. is mentioned, and Lord knows it is mentioned often, Lane becomes nostalgic, confidential, cynical. His point is that, when he was with the Agency in some exotic country, which he is not at liberty to name, the Agency was not even competent to arrange an abortion for a young, highly valued contact, whom, on that account, it lost. True or false, this anecdote evidently means a lot to Lane. He seems to find in it an immense, a universal relevance. "Guatemala," he'll say. "Don't tell me about Guatemala. When I was with the Agency, do you know we couldn't even arrange . . .," or "Clandestine activities. Don't make me laugh. When I was with the Agency, we couldn't even manage . . ." Apart from Lane, though, we all regard as fraught, and even graceless, allusions to such personal concerns as race, religion, income, politics, sexual proclivities, and now: institutional affiliation.

"Are you shaky on ladders?" Jim said. It had crossed my mind just then. I had never been shaky on ladders in my life before. I looked down the three flights of ladders to the cement floor. I laughed. "Hell, no," I said. "Not at all." "It would be O.K.," he said. "Fears are such a personal thing." I would not have been scared, I think, if I had been wearing sneakers and jeans. But climbing around a construction site in high heels and all, I was beset by an extreme proposition of What if. What if I just cleave to the rungs and hover here, without looking down at the concrete. Nothing could be done. If Jim were to hold out his hand from the rungs above, it wouldn't help; if I leaned back, the entire ladder would probably fall. The thing is to eradicate the What if, or at least postpone it, until it becomes an appropriate, theoretical speculation, on the stable ground.

The idea of hostages is very deep. Becoming pregnant is taking a hostage—as is running a pawnshop, being a bank, receiving a letter, taking a photograph, or listening to a confidence. Every love story, every commercial trade, every secret, every matter in which trust is involved, is a gentle transaction of hostages. Everything is, to a degree, in the custody of every other thing. Blackmail, kidnapping, then, are among the extreme violations of the deal. Anyway, I seem to be about to have Jim's child; at least, I think I will, and the thing is I haven't mentioned it to Jim.

"Far from it." There he is again. "Don't dwell on it."

In any group of two or more, it seems, somebody is on trial. Sometimes more than one person is on trial. Sometimes everyone is. But not for long. Under the law, a person can be said to plan alone or to plot alone, but not to conspire alone. There are other things, of course, no one can do alone: be a mob, or a choir, or a regiment. Or elope.

We had been heading for it all afternoon. Every time we all decide to do something out of doors, we begin the day with a sense of exuberant good health, followed by a slow intoxication of danger. Often it ends mildly. Somebody barefoot steps on broken glass, or one of the beer drinkers cuts himself on the tin. One year, somebody's guest from Palo Alto actually inhaled a cinder of his marijuana. Other times, someone missteps serving at tennis, falls, turns gray. In every case, it winds up in the emergency room. When this happens, it is always past four in the afternoon. Whoever is hurt, if he is conscious, apologizes. The form is from school days. The boy who got carsick and made the school bus stop, the girl who had a tantrum and then high fevers on the way to the museum, always spoke of spoiling it for everyone. Counting the wounded at the end of an afternoon these days, as they still apologize for spoiling it for everybody, we often find that the wounded outnumber the one or two hale whom they seem to think they have spoiled it for.

When Dan rode his bicycle over a cliff, we all behaved in characteristic ways. We were in Central Park. There was intense competition for calm, for sane instructions. Cover him, take his pulse, call a doctor, get an ambulance, stand back, raise his head, don't move him, leave him room and air. He had been riding his bicycle at full speed, with a kind of Western-yodel whoop, over the cliff edge. It had been a dare. He was out quite cold. In the rush to help, Jeff and Lee—who are the nicest of us, really—quietly returned all the bicycles, including Dan's, with its bent frame and mangled wheel, to the store from which we had rented them for the day. Two uniformed men appeared. They told Dan to get up. He opened his eyes. "Lie still," we said. "Wait for the ambulance." One of the uniformed men said, "Hey, man, we *are* the ambulance." Dan blinked. He tottered up a steep hill to their car. He sat on a stretcher. They let him sit up, occasionally bumping his head lightly against the roof, all the way to the hospital. He mumbled apologies. Ralph's girl, in a helpless daze of solicitude, held Dan's shoe in her lap. Situps aside, it is possible that we are really a group of invalids, hypochondriacs, and misfits. I don't know. Even our people who stay fit with yoga seem to be, more than others, subject to the flu.

"Do you realize how angry you sound?" must be one of the most infuriating questions in the language. "Good morning," says the poet's wife, quite sunny-natured. "Do you realize," the poet replies, "how angry you sound?" The poet's wife, confused, pacific, says she isn't at all angry. He repeats his question. Three more disclaimers on her part; on his, three more apparently calm and deadpan repetitions, and she is in fact beside herself. We are all, from time to time, too—well, too vehement. But there doesn't seem to be much anger in our set. Nor much of the happy faculty of saying, This is mine, and this is mine, and this too is mine, by right. When it is not. In the idiom of our class and generation, we said, Maybe we could lie down for a minute.

On a charter flight, I once met a middle-aged black man from Georgia, who had served in World War II, put himself through school, and then through college in the South. His oldest son had won a scholarship to Yale. At the end of his junior year, the son dropped out. He was going to travel across the country, play the guitar, and find himself. In less than twenty years, in short, and by an accident of historic time, that family had lived through the whole circle of the dream, in which the sons throw away what it has been the sole hope and effort of the grandfathers to amass and to consolidate. Shirtsleeves to shirtsleeves in one generation, in these times, perhaps. Or the boy might become a star and send all his own sons to Yale.

Jim has in his mind, I think, one erratically ringing alarm clock, one manacled dervish, one dormouse, replete with truisms, and one jurist with a clarity of such an order that I tend to love his verdict in most things. So, there is the question of this hostage, if that's what it is, and there is the fact of my not having mentioned it to him. These days, Jim says, very often, "Well, I had to make a decision. In my judgment, it was the right one; I'll stand by it." Every politician seems to like to say that. I don't care for it. Having somebody's children is not, of course, the sort of thing that yields much to consultation. There it is. One simply does it. On the other hand, there seems to me no time, simply no time, even years from now, when such a decision is not subject to review. Leaving aside the more gothic possibilities, what if one's son (or, and this seems unimaginable, daughter) simply, from the first and in every way, doesn't turn out right, or is unhappy all his life, what then? I don't know what then. "You can't miss it" always means you're never going to find it. The shortest distance between two points may well be the wrong way on a one way street. All the same, all the same, I think there's something to be said for assuring the next that the water's fine—quite warm, actually—once you get into it. You can't miss it. It could be that the sort of sentence one wants right here is the kind that runs, and laughs, and slides, and stops right on a dime.